THE DOOR FROM NOWHERE

Jay Ashton was born in Essex and now lives in Wales.
She has also lived in Uganda and France. She has
always been fascinated by nature, is very active in local
conservation groups, and gets enormous pleasure from
watching the wildlife around her. She has a son, and
says she cannot live without a cat around.

LOOKING FOR ILYRIAND

The Door from Nowhere

Jay Ashton

PUFFIN BOOKS

PUFFIN BOOKS

Published by the Penguin Group
Penguin Books Ltd, 27 Wrights Lane, London W8 5TZ, England
Penguin Books USA Inc., 375 Hudson Street, New York, New York 10014, USA
Penguin Books Australia Ltd, Ringwood, Victoria, Australia
Penguin Books Canada Ltd, 10 Alcorn Avenue, Toronto, Ontario, Canada M4V 3B2
Penguin Books (NZ) Ltd, 182–190 Wairau Road, Auckland 10, New Zealand

Penguin Books Ltd, Registered Offices: Harmondsworth, Middlesex, England

First published by Oxford University Press 1992
Published in Puffin Books 1993
1 3 5 7 9 10 8 6 4 2

Printed in England by Clays Ltd, St Ives plc
Filmset in Plantin

For my son Nick
with love

Author's Note

Swansea is of course real enough, but this story is pure invention. The only character in the book with a real-life model is Barkis the dog. For this I hope he will forgive me.

Cerian is pronounced Kerryan.

I am grateful for the financial assistance of the Welsh Arts Council which enabled me to write this book.

CHAPTER ONE
Wednesday 17 July

It was the last day of term. Cerian took a short cut past the deserted farm.

Normally she avoided going home that way. Today, loaded with books and kit and the products of projects, she decided to take the risk.

Her best friends were all going away on holiday and she was afraid she was going to be bored.

She picked her way up the sunken lane, wincing as she turned her ankle on a treacherous rock. The high banks on either side were thick with hazel and hawthorn and the branches met overhead, cutting out the light. It was almost like being underground.

She tiptoed past the tumbledown farmhouse under its shroud of ivy and heaved a sigh of relief.

As she went past the cowshed it groaned.

For one heart-stopping moment she froze. Then she fled. She was over the gate, up the hill and through the next field before she stopped running. She felt rather stupid then. It was of course her imagination. Still . . .

She had dropped most of her stuff but there was no way she was going back, not without Barkis for protection.

The lock on the front door was stiff and the key refused to turn. Eventually it gave and she fell through into the hall. 'I'm home!' she yelled. Silence.

She wandered through to the pottery, found her father painting a bloodstain on a garden gnome. 'I'm home,' she said again.

'Mmm.'

There was no point in talking to him while he was in that sort of mood.

Barkis heaved himself to his feet and lumbered behind her back to the kitchen, looking plaintive. His St Bernard bulk was never satisfied.

There were only three biscuits in the tin. Cerian shared them with Barkis, then fetched his lead. The dog's face fell even lower. He hated walks.

He hated cows too.

The third field was full of them, just out from milking.

Barkis sat on his ample behind and refused to move.

'Come *on*!' begged Cerian. 'You're supposed to be protecting me.' She shooed the cows, who moved reluctantly to one side. Equally reluctantly Barkis walked on.

Two more fields. The buildings of the abandoned farm stood dark and silent.

Cerian took a deep breath as she opened the gate.

No one around. No sound but birdsong.

Suddenly the dog barked, shattering the silence. Growling, hackles raised, he stalked into the cowshed.

'Barkis!' she called. 'Here! *Barkis!*' No response. Swallowing hard, she followed the dog into the shed.

There was a boy sitting on the ground laughing as Barkis licked his face.

'He hates strangers,' said Cerian.

'He likes me.'

'You're no good, dog.' Cerian, made to feel foolish, felt angry. 'Why don't you bite him?'

'Why should he?'

'Pretending you're a ghost. I dropped all my stuff.'

'The ghosts aren't in here. They're in the house.'

'You're crazy.' She still felt cross. 'What are you doing here anyway?'

'It's a secret. No one's supposed to know. That's why I tried to frighten you off.' The boy pushed Barkis away and stood up. He was just the same height as Cerian, with light hair that fell into his eyes and lots of grooves about his face. Cerian couldn't decide whether he was ugly or good-looking. In the end she thought he was ugly but looked good.

2

'You won't tell on me, will you?' he asked.

' . . . No. My name's Cerian. What's yours?'

He hesitated. 'Dylan,' he said finally.

'You don't sound Welsh.'

'I am too.' Indignant.

'But you're not from here?'

'I've come back.'

Barkis was snuffling round the shed. Cerian followed him with her eyes, saw a sleeping-bag and rucksack. 'You're not *sleeping* in here?' She was awestruck.

Dylan shrugged. 'It's all right.'

'How long have you been here?'

'Since yesterday.'

'And how long are you going to stay?'

'As long as it takes.'

'As long as what takes?'

'I'm . . . I'm looking for someone.'

'Well, you can't stay here.' She spoke with conviction. 'There's no roof, the ground's filthy and how are you going to eat—and what about washing?'

'You sound like someone's mother.'

'You look like you need a mother.'

He went very still.

'Have you run away from home?' demanded Cerian.

'You won't tell, will you? Promise you won't tell.'

'Why have you run away?'

'That's a secret too. Anyway, you wouldn't believe me if I told you.'

'How old are you?'

'Thirteen.'

Cerian smiled from the superiority of fourteen. 'Come to tea,' she said.

Dylan hesitated, then said, 'All right.'

'Don't strain yourself,' said Cerian. She stopped outside the cowshed to pick up her school things.

Barkis sniffed the air, then began to walk stiff-legged, head lowered, towards the farmhouse.

Dylan grabbed his collar. 'Not in there,' he said.

Barkis just carried on walking, dragging Dylan with him. 'Cerian, help.'

School kit clutched under one arm, she too caught the dog's collar. 'Why? What's in the farmhouse?'

Dylan's eyes met hers over Barkis's broad back. 'Told you,' he said. 'Ghosts.'

'I don't believe in ghosts,' said Cerian, not altogether truthfully.

'Neither do I,' said Dylan. But his eyes slid away.

Barkis waddled into the kitchen and subsided with a hard-done-by air. There was a delicious garlicky smell.

'Finished the gnomes then?' asked Cerian.

'Uh-huh.' Her father, busy slicing carrots into the pan, didn't look round.

'This is Dylan.'

'Hello, Dylan. Tom Rhys. Call me Tom.' He transferred a carrot into his left hand and held out his right.

Dylan shook it. Tom was big and bearded and comfortable.

'You've come to tea? I hope you like soup?'

'There's always soup,' said Cerian.

'It's good stuff,' said Tom.

'I love soup,' said Dylan politely.

'Come on, Mulligan.' Cerian moved a half-grown marmalade cat off the table and went to fetch a cloth. The cat had jumped back up by the time she turned round again.

'He's nice,' said Dylan, offering his fingers to be sniffed. 'I like cats.'

'He's a she,' said Cerian.

'I thought all ginger cats were males.'

'They usually are. All except Mulligan.'

Cerian moved the cat a second time and spread the cloth over the table. By the time she had fetched spoons and knives Mulligan was back. She gave up and started to lay the table round her.

'What's in here?' asked Dylan, peering into a vast aquarium which took up most of the windowsill.

'All sorts,' said Tom. 'Know anything about pond life?' Abandoning the soup, he took the lid off the aquarium and began to point out caddis fly larvae, mayfly nymphs and water-boatmen.

The soup threatened to boil over. Cerian stirred it.

'I won a prize for my nature project,' said Dylan.

'Well done,' said Tom. 'Hey, look at this. The hydra, see? It's caught a cyclops.'

'Do you want these beans in the soup?' asked Cerian.

'Mmm. I bet you don't know what these are.'

'Snail eggs,' said Dylan.

'How much parsley?' asked Cerian.

'Oh . . . I'll do it.' Reluctantly Tom returned to the stove, pushing Mulligan off the table as he passed. The cat jumped for her favourite perch on the aquarium.

There was a loud splash. Mulligan rose vertically through the air, spraying duckweed, landed on a shelf and dislodged a jar which crashed to the ground in a welter of lentils.

'Look at that, he's made the tank all muddy,' said Tom indignantly.

Cerian fetched a dustpan and brush and started sweeping up the lentils.

By the time the mess was cleared up the soup was ready.

They sat down to eat. Dylan wondered who the fourth place was laid for.

The door crashed open. A woman staggered in and fell into a chair, dropping a bulging briefcase by her side.

'God, what a day,' she moaned.

'Soup, Bea?' asked Tom.

'Hello, Mum,' said Cerian. 'This is Dylan.'

'Hello, Dylan,' said Bea mechanically. 'Any phone calls for me?'

'Dunno,' said Tom. 'Phone rang while I was working. I didn't answer it.'

'Damn,' said Bea. 'I wonder who that was?'

It was good soup. Dylan ate hungrily.

Barkis moved around the table, laying his head in people's laps and looking hopeful. He was drooling beguilingly at Dylan when the door opened and in came an old lady carrying a set of golf clubs. Barkis greeted her with enthusiasm.

'Evening, Mamgu,' said Tom. 'Off out?'

'I'm playing a round with Sylvia. All right if I take the van?'

'Fine.' Tom passed over the keys.

'This is Dylan,' said Cerian.

'Good evening, Dylan.' The old lady shook his hand formally. 'Are you here on holiday?'

'Yes,' said Cerian, while Dylan hesitated.

'I mustn't stop. I don't want to keep Sylvia waiting.' The old lady went out, followed by Barkis.

'Have a nice time,' called Bea, still immersed in her papers.

'What did you call her?' asked Dylan. 'Mamgee?'

'That's right,' said Tom. 'M-a-m-hard g-u. It's the Welsh for Grandma. Have you finished? Would you like to see the pottery?'

The pottery smelt damp and dusty. At one end stood an enormous kiln. There were shelves heaped with sacks and bags, and more shelves on which stood row upon row of garden gnomes, some undecorated still, some painted.

Looking closer Dylan realized all the gnomes were dead. Some seemed to have been hit by a blunt instrument, some had a noose round the neck or a dagger in the back.

'I bet you're wondering why,' said Tom. 'Thing is, the garden centre down the road asked me to make them twelve dozen gnomes. I hate the things personally, but I wanted the money. I made the moulds, turned out a gross of gnomes, painted and glazed. Then the garden centre said they didn't want them. Could get them cheaper from Hong Kong. I came home and murdered the lot. Hung them from the apple trees, floated them in the pond, laid them around with their heads broken off. Some friends saw them, wanted some. Then their friends . . . Suddenly everyone wants dead gnomes. I have to spend my whole life making gnomes and murdering them. Here, this is what I really like doing.'

He reached up to a top shelf and brought down a tiny sculpture of toadstools, grass and a butterfly. 'Porcelain, that is. Takes days to make one. Nobody will pay the price. Dead gnomes, that's all they want.'

The sun was setting as Dylan walked back across the fields. To his left the lights of Swansea slipped down into the sea, where a lighthouse pulsed. He turned right at the top of the ridge, down into the darkness. Cwm Rhithiol, Cerian had called it: Valley of Shadows. He shivered, remembering, then slowly headed downhill, back to his cowshed.

He went to pee in the bushes, then stopped, listening. The moonlight was cold, the darkness thick as treacle. Something tapped. Maybe a bramble in the wind. But there was no wind. Overhead, patches of blackness flitted silent against the stars. Bats. The doorway to the farmhouse yawned open, calling. Just beyond the stretch of his hearing were the voices, scratching at the back of his mind. 'Not now,' he whispered.

He ran into the cowshed, shivered down inside the sleeping-bag, closed his ears to the whispering.

CHAPTER TWO

Thursday 18 July

'Your family's weird,' said Dylan.

Cerian admitted it. 'I do my best with them, but . . . ' She sighed.

'Thanks for not telling them—about me running away, I mean.'

'I never betray a secret,' said Cerian virtuously. 'Anyway, they probably wouldn't take any notice,' she added more honestly.

Dylan grinned. She looked older out of school uniform, wearing jeans and a black 'Friends of the Earth' sweatshirt. She reminded him of an otter, with her short dark hair slicked back and bright, friendly eyes in a roundish face.

'So,' she said. 'Tell me. Why did you run away?'

Dylan's smile evaporated. There was a long pause.

'Did you know there's a badger sett in the woods?' he asked eventually.

'No—where? How do you know?'

'I found it. Yesterday. Do you want to see?'

'Yes, please.' He hadn't answered her question, but Cerian was prepared to wait. Sooner or later he'd spit it out.

She smiled encouragingly and let him lead her into the wood.

With hardly a pause Dylan pushed his way through the undergrowth, ducking under branches and twisting round brambles, till he picked up a faint path. It was wide enough to follow, but too low: it kept diving underneath obstacles instead of going round them.

'The path's made by badgers,' he said. 'They follow the same tracks, one badger after another, for hundreds of years. Here, look.'

He bent down to where a stout bramble lay across the

path. Caught on a spike was a little tuft of hair striped grey and cream and tipped with black.

'You know a lot about them,' said Cerian.

'Sure.' He held the bramble back for her to pass, then led on.

Just at the edge of the wood, where the trees thinned before giving way to grassy fields, there was a sandy bank. 'Here,' he said. 'Here's one hole—and another here—and another over there . . . '

He scrambled around the bank, pointing out the tree where badgers sharpened their claws, the pile of used bedding.

'No prints, though,' he said. 'It's been too dry.'

He sat down by one of the holes. Cerian sat beside him. 'How do you know all this?' she asked.

'My mum . . . she takes—took—me for walks. Only she's not really my mum,' he added in a rush.

Cerian looked at him.

He picked up a twig and started tracing patterns in the dust. 'I thought she was till a couple of weeks ago.' He went on staring at the ground. 'I was looking in her desk for an envelope and I found this letter. It was sealed up but it was addressed to me. At least it had my name on it. So I read it.'

He fell silent.

A blackbird scuffled under a bush, turning over the dead leaves.

'It was from a social worker. About where I really came from. Who my real parents are.'

He flushed, stumbling over the words. 'I'm il—illegitimate. My real mother had—you know. I mean—she left her husband and went to this other man and then she had me, only by then she'd gone back to her husband and she gave me away.'

His lip trembled.

'Oh,' said Cerian.

Dylan started to break the twig into smaller and smaller pieces. 'So I sealed the letter up again and put it back. And then everything kept going wrong and my mum kept getting cross with me and I lost my coat again and then I had a really big row with my dad, so I ran away.'

'To find your real mother?' guessed Cerian.

'Yes. So I could tell her what I think of her,' said Dylan. Cerian looked sideways at him.

'She's a cow,' said Dylan defiantly. 'I mean, I didn't *ask* to be born. It's not my fault. And she just gave me away. Thanks very much!'

There were tears in his eyes. Cerian thought it better not to notice. 'Is your name really Dylan?'

'It is now. I mean, they called me Simon and pretended I was English, but really I'm Welsh and Dylan's what my real mum called me.'

'Where does she live?'

'I don't know, only that it's Swansea. I thought it would be easy enough when I left London—I thought, Swansea's only a small place. All the way here on the coach I was thinking I'd only have to look her up in the phone book . . .'

'What's her name?'

'Hughes. There's *pages* of them . . . ' Dylan fell silent, remembering. He'd been expecting a little seaside town, with pink cottages along a beach, not a city like London, all crowds and traffic. He'd seen himself walking up the path, his rucksack on his back and his mother throwing open her arms to him. Dreams were always better. They used to tell him off at school for not paying attention, but really he was proud of his daydreams. His English teacher said he had a lot of imagination. He used to imagine rescuing people from a burning building or winning the Derby to escape from a boring history lesson or to get himself asleep at night. Now he felt a bit better, seeing himself as the hero of his own story.

'Don't you know her first name?' asked Cerian.

'She's Catherine Elizabeth Hughes.'

'There you are then. Easy.'

'Ye-es—but phones are always listed under the man's name, aren't they?. And I don't know what he's called. I didn't know what to do so I just got on the first bus that came and stayed on it till I saw some countryside. I thought I'd be bound to find a barn or something. So I fetched up here—night before last, that was—and yesterday I just spent exploring the woods and I still don't know what to do.' He didn't mention the ghosts in the farmhouse. He didn't want to think about them.

'Right,' said Cerian, standing up. 'I'll help. Come on.'

'Where to?'

'The library. You've just moved to Swansea, mind, and you want to find a girl you met on holiday. You know her name but not her address.'

'A *girl*? Why not a boy?'

Cerian grinned. 'Because they'll be more helpful if they think it's a girl you're looking for. Must be all the romances they spend their time with!'

But they didn't get to the library, not that day.

When they called at Cerian's house to get pens and paper, Tom was loading boxes into the back of a van. 'Come on, you two,' he called. 'I've got a delivery on Gower. It's a lovely day. We'll have a picnic on the beach.'

Dylan, postponing his search with a feeling of relief, helped with the loading. The van was old, battered, and had 'Tom Rhys—Dead Gnomes' painted on the side and 'Don't Panic' on the back.

With some persuasion and a lot of pushing they managed to get Barkis into the back, locked the door on him, then squashed into the front.

Tom's driving was calm, steady and unhurried, though he rarely stopped for red lights. Dylan closed his eyes several times but magically they sailed through junctions unscathed.

They passed an airfield, with cows all over the road, then the lane closed in, winding up and down hill, trees either side. Slowing down they came to a row of houses with huge front gardens. One was laid out with streams, waterfalls, temples and bridges, just like a willow-pattern plate except

11

that everywhere—fishing, sunbathing, standing chatting—were plastic garden gnomes.

Tom drove past, and turned into the drive of the house next door.

A woman came out, smiling. 'You've brought them! Henry will be pleased! He'll be down in a minute.'

As Tom opened the door of the van, Barkis fell out and sat in an indignant heap on the drive. They unloaded the boxes and Tom unpacked the contents: twenty-four murdered gnomes.

'I'll let Henry arrange them,' said the woman. 'He's been so looking forward to this. Our neighbour's been driving him mad—I mean, have you ever seen anything like it?' They gazed over the fence at the cascades and pavilions. The plastic gnomes glared back.

'Just you wait,' said the woman to a large red gnome sitting on a toadstool. 'Oh, here's Henry.'

'Magnificent!' cried Henry. 'Sorry to keep you waiting. I was just finishing my sermon.' He was tall and plump and his face, over his clerical collar, shone with unholy glee.

They parked where the road ended and walked down a narrow track between hedges alive with butterflies. It opened out on to a grassy clifftop, the coast stretching out in a series of bays and headlands, the sun dazzling on the sea.

The path wound down through gorse bushes that sparkled with yellow flowers. More butterflies, shimmering on the heady air.

The beach was sandy, smooth and almost deserted. Barkis limped to the nearest rock-pool and sat in it, panting.

'Right then,' said Tom. 'A dip before lunch.'

Dylan hesitated. 'I haven't got any trunks.'

'Trunks?' said Tom. 'Oh, you mean bathers. Wear your underpants, they'll dry after. Last one in's a cissy.' He made as if to start running, then dropped behind as Dylan and Cerian raced neck and neck.

It was a dead heat to the chill, blue, wave-tossing wonderful sea.

'Dylan,' said Cerian, swallowing a mouthful of peanut butter sandwich. 'Tell me about the ghosts in the farmhouse.'

He was silent, looking down the beach to where Tom lay sleeping. 'It was the evening I arrived,' he said eventually. 'I saw the buildings from the top of the hill, thought they'd be a good place to sleep. I looked in the cowshed first, then the pigsty—I didn't fancy that much.' He paused. 'It was just getting dark. The door at the front of the house was blocked, so I went round to the side . . . I can't explain it, I just . . . There was something there—voices, only I couldn't quite hear them. I had this feeling they were waiting for me. Like they wanted to get at me. I dunno. All sounds pretty stupid, doesn't it?'

'No,' said Cerian, considering. 'It's a spooky place. I mean, I don't believe in ghosts, of course, only there's supposed to have been some sort of tragedy there, I don't know what. Maybe we could find out.'

'*No*,' said Dylan. 'I don't want to.'

'All right, have it your own way. Do you like caves?'

She led him on a hectic scramble up and down rocks, past the next bay, over the headland and down to a jagged slit in the cliff. The entrance to the cave was over great slippery boulders. Dylan slithered over them, then paused. There was a vast empty space disappearing into darkness. He turned and looked back to the mouth of the cave. The rocks were black and glistening, the sky and the sea white and shining behind a screen of waterdrops that glinted as they fell.

The light left patterns in his eyes as he turned back to the dark. Cerian had vanished.

'There were mammoths here,' said her disembodied voice, suddenly loud from the back of the cave. 'And rhinoceroses, and lions and hippos.'

'Are you having me on?' Dylan picked his way over the slippery rocks to join her.

'No, really. Some archaeologists came from the British Museum. They said the bones had been brought in by hyenas. And people used to live here, too.'

'Cavemen.'

'Mmm. Thousands of years ago, in the Iron Age, then the Celts hid here from the Romans, then the Saxons hid here from the Vikings.'

Dylan imagined men in tunics cowering, as through the cave entrance they saw dragon boats approaching. At least it would be easy to defend. The enemy would have to scramble up the rocks one by one, using their hands to climb. Easy prey for bows and arrows or boiling oil. He saw himself as a Celtic chieftain, leading his men in battle against the invaders.

'So when were the Welsh?' he asked.

'What do you mean?'

'All those different sorts of people—where do the Welsh fit in?'

Cerian thought. 'I don't know really. I suppose they're made up of all of them.'

Dylan felt confused. It seemed to be more complicated than he'd thought, being Welsh.

It was seven o'clock before they got back. There was a smell of cooking in the hall.

'Oh no,' said Cerian. 'Mum's getting dinner.'

'Is that bad?' asked Dylan.

'Could be. She experiments.'

The smell intensified as they went into the kitchen.

'Hello, Dylan,' said Bea. 'Are you stopping for dinner? There's plenty to go round.'

'Thank you very much,' said Dylan.

'That was well timed,' said Bea. 'It's nearly ready.' She stirred a saucepan vigorously.

Cerian started laying the table. Tom poured himself a beer. Dylan slumped in a chair, feeling the sun still on his skin.

14

Suddenly an alarm bell shrilled. Tom, Bea and Cerian turned as one and shot towards the door.

'What is it?' cried Dylan, running after them.

'Mamgu!' shouted Cerian.

They all hurtled up the stairs, the dog labouring in pursuit, barking deafeningly. Past the first floor, up to the second; Bea in the lead hurled open the door. Dylan had a brief glimpse of orange fur and a bottle-brush tail as the cat shot out and vanished down the stairs.

Bea stopped dead. They all piled into each other.

'Your cat,' said Mamgu, moistening her paint-brush, 'pulled the alarm cord.'

Dylan stared. Mamgu was sitting at a huge table which was laid out with hills and valleys and opposing armies. She held a green-and-scarlet figure on which she was painting gold braid.

'Wretched animal!' said Bea. 'My sauce will have gone all lumpy.' She headed back downstairs, tripping over Barkis who, late but determined, staggered into the room, growling.

'Not seen the likes of this before, have you?' said Tom, clapping Dylan on the shoulder. 'Shut up, Barkis.'

'It's the Battle of Waterloo,' said Mamgu. 'French here, British there, Prussians late of course, right over there . . . '

'I think dinner's ready,' said Cerian. 'Barkis, do be quiet.'

'Do you know your military history, Dylan?' asked Mamgu. 'Napoleon should have won, only the Imperial Guard—'

'No so, Mamgu,' said Tom, 'I keep telling you that Blücher—'

'We have to go,' interrupted Cerian, pulling Dylan towards the door. 'Come on, Dad, *dinner.*'

Dylan followed her downstairs. Tom and Mamgu were still arguing. The dog's growls erupted into barking: it sounded as if he was joining in.

In the hall, Cerian stopped to turn the bell off. In the sudden silence their ears seemed to be still ringing.

Bea was dishing dinner as they walked into the kitchen.

'What is it?' asked Dylan nervously.

'Falafel with garlic sauce,' said Bea, starting to eat.

'More garlic,' said Cerian.

'Good for you,' said Bea. 'Wards off evil spirits.'

Dylan looked up. 'Really?'

'Of course. Why, are you bothered by them?'

'Oh no,' he said quickly.

Tom had not returned. His dinner sat congealing slowly.

'Not from here, are you, Dylan?' asked Bea.

'He's on holiday,' said Cerian.

'Oh? Where are you staying?'

'With friends,' said Cerian. 'Down by the school.'

'Let him talk, Cerian. So where are you from, Dylan?'

'London.'

'Are you staying long?'

'Don't know.'

'You'd never guess what we saw on the beach,' said Cerian.

'Oh, what?'

Dylan, grateful for the distraction, concentrated on his food. It wasn't bad once he got used to it, and if it would keep off evil spirits . . .

Dylan woke in the dark, the sweet animal smell catching at the back of his throat. It was very warm. All around he could hear snorts and chewing and the low breathing of cattle.

He sat up: the shed was empty and silent in the moonlight.

16

CHAPTER THREE

Friday 19 July

Cerian led the way up stone steps and through a frosted-glass door marked 'Reference Library'. Dylan followed reluctantly, wishing he had never started this, nervous of what he might discover, worried he might be found out.

'Can I help you?' The librarian did not look too frightening: plump, glasses, green dress.

'We're looking for someone,' said Cerian. 'This is my cousin. He's just moved to Swansea and he wants to find this girl he met on holiday.'

'Do you know her address?'

Dylan shook his head.

'Well, there's the phone book. What you can do is look up the name—you do know her name?—then check with the electoral register.'

'What's that?' asked Cerian.

The librarian smiled. She was quite nice really. 'It's a list, street by street, of everybody who is registered to vote. Although I expect this girl is under eighteen? So she wouldn't be listed.'

'I know her mother's name,' said Dylan quickly.

'Fine. So what you'll have to do is look up in the phone book everyone in Swansea with the right name, and copy down the addresses. Then you show me the list and I'll find you the right sections of the electoral register. You look up the street and it'll give you the full names of all the voters who live there. Oh—she has been here since last October?'

Dylan nodded.

'Or there is another way—you tell me who you're looking for, and I can write to the people who maintain the register. They have an alphabetical list and they can look it up, then write to the person and ask if she minds being contacted by you. If she says it's all right, then we can give you the address.'

'I think we'd rather do it ourselves,' said Cerian.

'As you like. I hope it's not too common a name?'

'It's Hughes,' said Cerian.

'Could be better, could be worse. If it was Jones it would take you weeks!'

They sat side by side at a big wooden table with the phone book between them. Cerian set to work straight away, copying from the left-hand page, running her finger down the telephone numbers till she came to a Swansea entry then copying down the address. Dylan wrote down two addresses from the right-hand page, then stopped to look around.

The room was circular, with a gallery halfway up the walls and, high above, a dome painted green, white and orange. The gallery was lined with bookshelves, rounded to fit the walls; there were shiny brass handles, each with a duster tucked through. The books were all dark brown and ancient looking. There was nobody up there.

Downstairs, though, was crowded, with people sitting at every table. Students, mostly, and men reading newspapers. There was a girl working her way through all the volumes of Yellow Pages. A man in a sleeveless pullover and shapeless hat peered at a big leather-bound book. There was a ginger-haired man writing, who looked up frequently: Dylan kept catching his eye.

There was a humming noise from the heating system, the rustling of pages turning, the murmur of the staff behind the desk. Someone dropped a pen, the phone warbled and someone coughed.

Racks around the room appealed: 'Please take a leaflet!'

Two marble busts: no one Dylan recognized, but labelled. 'Who's *Dim Ysmygu*?' he whispered. 'Stupid name!'

Cerian giggled. 'Stupid yourself! It's the Welsh for No Smoking.'

18

Dylan flushed and went back to work.

This time he got halfway down the column before he stopped. The addresses were mostly places like Brynhyfryd and Cwmbwrla and he kept losing his place.

There were four and five eighths pages of Hughes. He counted down a column: 130 names. Three columns per page: $390 \times 4\frac{5}{8}$ was 1,805, more or less. Over 1,800 Hughes to work through. He sighed, looked up and met the ginger man's eyes again. Did he suspect? Perhaps he was a plain-clothes policeman. Were they looking for him at home? Not they, they'd be glad he'd gone, they'd never wanted him, kept saying he was a nuisance.

Cerian jogged his arm. 'Come on, you're awfully slow.'

'There's so many of them,' complained Dylan. 'Do you know there's over 1,800 Hughes?'

'Well, you won't get it done by staring at the wall.'

Dylan sighed and picked up his pen again. At least they didn't all live in Swansea. There were . . . twenty-four Swansea numbers in the column, twenty-four times fourteen columns would be 336 addresses to look up in the electoral register. This was going to take for ever. He was sure the ginger-haired man was looking at them suspiciously. 'We could do this at your house,' he whispered.

'But then we'd have to come back to look at the register.'

'It's going to take us all day to do this anyway.'

'All right, only let me get to the bottom of this column. I don't want to lose my place.'

Bon-y-Maen, Ynystawe, Cwmrhydyceirw . . . Dim Ysmygu, funny words. He ought to learn the language, since he was Welsh.

'Is Welsh difficult?'

'Ssh!'

It was soup again for supper: Tom cooked.

Cerian had told her parents, with her fingers crossed behind her back, that Dylan was the only child of elderly parents who slept all the time, and he found it much more interesting to be with her. So they made no comment on his

19

presence, for which he was grateful. He was hungry: he'd had nothing all day since his last chocolate bar for breakfast. Tomorrow he'd have to buy some food. Sausages would be nice, only he didn't have any way to cook them. And he wasn't sure how long £3.47 would last.

'Take Barkis for a walk, will you, kids?' asked Tom after supper. 'He needs some exercise.'

'I don't think he wants any,' said Dylan, trying to pull him to his feet.

'Come on, hound!' Tom slapped the St Bernard's vast behind and Barkis wallowed to his feet, growling.

The sun was low and had lost its bite. Cerian knotted her sweatshirt round her waist and enjoyed the slight evening chill on her bare arms.

They headed out through fields spangled with flowers and buzzing still with grasshoppers. Barkis waded through the grass ignoring the insects.

'I've never met a dog before that didn't like walks,' said Dylan.

Cerian laughed. 'He never has. Even when he was a puppy we had to drag him out. Mum got him because she wanted a big dog to go with her when she gets in a bad mood. When she's upset she walks miles. She still makes Barkis go with her, but he hates it. You can see him cringing when Mum and Dad have a row, thinking, oh no, not again.'

'Do they often have rows?' Dylan was shocked. Voices were rarely raised in his house.

'All the time. It doesn't mean anything. It's just the way they are.'

'I'm not going to get married. I mean, you don't have to.' Dylan fell silent, brooding. Grown-ups always told you to do things because they knew best and then they went and mucked things up themselves.

They went through a gate, closing it behind them, and turned down a stony track. In the distance, down the hill, was the dark smudge of Cwm Rhithiol.

There was an old man sitting on the bank, an ancient

black retriever sniffing around him. The two dogs met noses, inspected back ends.

'A lovely evening,' said the man. One side of his face was twisted.

'Hello,' said Cerian. 'I think my dog likes yours.'

Half of the man's face smiled. 'Blackie likes everybody.' By his side was a walking stick, the top shaped into a deer's head.

'I like your stick,' said Dylan.

'I carve them myself. It's my hobby. I'm slow, though, these days. I look for likely branches this time of year, come back in December to cut them, when the sap's low. This one's holly. I didn't need to shape it much, it grew that way.'

'It's beautiful,' said Cerian.

The man did his best to smile again. 'Crab apple's good for sticks. Interesting nodes. You know what nodes are?'

'The bit where the leaf joins on,' said Dylan.

'That's right. They make a nice pattern. There's a wonderful tree in that hedge down there. And the fruit's magnificent this year! I've never seen such crabs. It'll all go if they build. They've got plans. More houses. More little boxes. I've lived here all my life, I've watched it all gradually disappear. Soon there'll be nothing left, only rows of little boxes.'

He fell silent. The sun was dipping low, flooding orange.

'You see that farmhouse down there?' the old man went on. Dylan jumped. 'I used to play there when I was a kid. It's been empty thirty years now. Two brothers, two sisters, there were. There's been a tragedy to all of them.' He sighed, shook his head.

Cerian looked at Dylan but he was staring down at the farmhouse. 'What happened?' she asked.

The old man sighed again. 'Owen, the eldest, he fell off a cliff on Gower. It was the other boy I used to play with, Howard. Played together all the time, we did. He's in and out of Cefn Coed now—that's the mental hospital—doesn't recognize me. I see him sometimes, he buys a can from the

21

off-licence and drinks it walking along. I said hello to him the other day, he just turned away, walks very fast he does, his head jerking backwards every little step. And the girls— the one died of consumption, the other, Megan . . . ' His voice trailed away.

'What happened to her?' asked Cerian.

'Hair like summer corn, she had, and a voice like an angel. Ran off when she was sixteen, never been seen again. Maybe she escaped. I hope so.'

'Escaped?'.

'Aye. They said, even when I was a kid, they said there was a curse on the place. Valley of Shadows, they call it, and there's been a shadow on everyone who lived there. My grandfather used to tell me tales . . . ' He shook his head.

All three stared down to where the sun had already left the valley. The ruined buildings were barely discernible in the gathering dark. 'Eerie, it is. I won't go there now.'

Cerian looked at Dylan. He avoided her eyes. 'What sort of curse?' she asked.

But the old man's eyes had glazed over. His dog came and laid its head in his lap.

'We should go,' said Dylan.

'Yes. Dark soon. You have a look as you go by, have a look at the crab apple, there's a branch there I'm keeping my eye on, make a lovely stick it will. Come on, Blackie, time we went home.'

They watched as the man and the dog went together down the track, limping. 'I said it was spooky,' said Cerian. 'Perhaps you really did see something.'

'I didn't *see* anything. But there's something . . . '

'Yes, well, rather you than me sleeping down there. Look, I'd better get home. Come round in the morning, we'll go back to the library.'

'I suppose so,' said Dylan. 'See you.'

He looked in the hedgerow as he passed, found the crab apple tree, heavy with fruit. He bit into one and spat it out. Sour. There was a long straight branch, maybe that was the one. Funny old man, with his walking sticks and curses.

22

In a defiant mood he jumped over the gate and marched up to the farmhouse, brushing through the nettles, pushing the brambles aside. But in the doorway he stopped.

It was nothing he could see or hear. But there was a thick feeling at the back of his throat and his skin crawled. 'What do you want?' he shouted suddenly. 'What do you want from me?'

There was no reply.

CHAPTER FOUR
Saturday 20 July

Dylan woke next morning with rain on his face. He huddled down, reluctant to move, then realized his sleeping-bag was getting wet. He crawled out, bundled up the bag and pushed it into a dry corner.

Nothing to eat. He'd go to the shop on the way to Cerian's.

Half past six, too early yet.

A grey mist filled the valley. The rain seemed not to be falling from the sky, but seeping upwards, sideways, in a fine soaking drizzle. A song thrush called hesitantly, then lapsed into silence.

He counted his money again. Still only £3.47. The coach had cost far more than he'd expected.

He slumped down in the doorway and stared at the falling mist. All the world had somewhere they belonged, except him. At home they'd still be in bed, fast asleep, not caring where he was, whether he was still alive. If he was dead, that would show them. Scenarios of accidents, fatal illnesses, rolled through his mind: how sorry they'd be, knowing it was all their fault.

And *she*, his real mother, having him, a little baby, and giving him to someone else because he was in the way. Babies were so cute, tiny little fingers and needing to be cuddled, she must be a—*witch*, a real *witch* to have done that.

So why had he come?

Hot tears and cold rain mingled on his cheeks.

Trotting, busy, tail flicking from side to side, a squirrel passed; paused by the door of the cowshed; looked at him, beady eyed; pattered on. Distracted despite his gloom, Dylan watched it go.

The squirrel went down the track, jigged to one side, vanished into the farmhouse. Dylan followed, the nettles slapping wet against his jeans.

He stood hesitating in the doorway.

The same thick feeling caught at the pit of his stomach. But there was something here he needed to find out. He stood his ground.

No door, no roof, most of upstairs lying tumbled to the ground. The floor was earth and ashes. Half-rotten timbers were stifled green with moss. One end of the room was in deep shadow cast by some first-floor boards still precariously in place. Above grew elder and sycamore.

The sky was neatly divided into squares by the framework of the vanished roof. Like prison bars, he thought, and shivered. Somewhere beyond his hearing, a voice seemed to be trying to reach him.

Opposite was the doorway to an inner room, around it a shower of ultramarine.

A wren chinked, flurried through what was once a window.

If it's all right for a bird, he thought . . . He walked forward into the house.

He sank to his ankles in the dust, stumbled over bricks lying hidden in the cinders. Brambles leaning from above caught at his clothes.

Dylan stooped to pick up one of the fragments of ultramarine. It was painted plaster. As he ran his finger over it the blue came off and stained his skin. Clutching it he stepped into the inner room.

Just over his head, a door opened from nowhere into nothing. Timbers lay diagonally, one end still clinging to the wall, the other fallen to the floor, heaped up around a stone hearth. The tendrils of brambles trailed almost to the ground.

This must be where the secret lay. The thick feeling intensified, solid at the back of his throat. Faces turned to him, demanding to be heard.

He twisted away and fled.

Dylan bought a Mars bar and two packets of cheese and onion crisps and ate them sitting on a wall, looking down towards the sea.

Almost everywhere in the town there was a view of the sea, so hilly it was. Narrow streets rose precipitously, allowing a sideways glimpse of glinting water. Terraces piled up on top of each other, open to the sky and the whole wide yawn of the bay, from the cranes in the dock to the lighthouse at Mumbles.

Why Mumbles? Silly name. He imagined all the inhabitants muttering darkly in each other's ears. Or did it mean something sensible in Welsh? Perhaps he'd get a book on Welsh out of the library. Only nobody here seemed to speak it—at least he hadn't heard anyone—there were just the road signs. Newport was Casnewydd and Swansea was Abertawe and 'intermittent hard shoulder' on the M4 was something long he'd forgotten.

Maybe he could get a job. A paper round or something. Under £3 left now. Still, something would turn up. It had to.

Cerian, Tom and Mulligan the cat were still eating breakfast when he arrived. 'There's some porridge left if you're hungry,' said Tom. Dylan hesitated. 'You might as well have it, it's you or Barkis and he's fat enough already.'

It wasn't Dylan's favourite food, but being wet and cold had made him hungry. As he ate, Barkis came and laid his head in Dylan's lap, drooling damply. Dylan left him some, scraping it into the bowl marked 'DOG'.

'That's Mulligan's dish,' said Cerian. Barkis ate it anyway.

Bea shot in, shuffling yet more papers into a briefcase already overflowing.

'Come on, you,' she said to the dog. 'I need a good long walk.' She picked up his lead and he looked depressed.

'Can you give us a lift to the library, Mum?' asked Cerian. 'Save us getting wet. Dylan's just starting to dry off.'

'All right. If you're ready now.'

Bea's car was an elderly Ford Escort. She persuaded Barkis into the front passenger seat while the children got into the back.

Bea drove off at high speed along the narrow streets. Barkis, his great bulk jolted from side to side, let out a low protesting howl. 'You're driving too fast,' said Cerian.

'Nonsense,' said her mother, nipping left, right and left again, in and out of approaching traffic. 'You don't get anywhere by hanging around.'

'There's a police car,' said Dylan.

Bea slowed down.

It was a different librarian at the desk this time. Cerian told the story again while Dylan fiddled with the microfiche catalogue. They had finished the list, copied from the phone book, of all the Hugheses they wanted to check out. The librarian, who was quite young and very friendly, helped them with the first few addresses, showing them how to look up the codes, find the right book, then locate the street. 'You're sensible kids,' she said after a while, 'I'll let you have the books and you can do it yourselves. You'll be careful with them, won't you?'

'Of course,' said Cerian, looking responsible.

Staggering under the weight of some fifteen fat directories, they took over one of the large tables in the corner and set to work. There were—Dylan had counted—319 addresses to check. Although, of course, Catherine Elizabeth might be married to an Anthony or an Andrew or an Albert and it might be the first entry they looked at. Or a William or a Walter or a Zachariah and then it would take ages. Or she might have moved away and they wouldn't find her at all. Better not to think of that. Except that Dylan was less and less sure that he wanted to find her. Except that he had to.

'Come on,' said Cerian, 'concentrate.'

'Sorry.' He read out the next address and Cerian leafed through the pages.

'Alun Michael Hughes, Jennifer Margaret Hughes, Matthew John Hughes . . . Next?'

And so it went on, whispered names, the quiet rustling as the pages turned, and no sign of Catherine. By eleven o'clock they had worked through twenty-three addresses and Dylan was wriggling.

'Got to find a toilet,' he whispered, and went off.

Cerian carried on, next address, find the code, find the right directory, find the street . . . After about ten minutes she looked up, wondering where Dylan had got to.

He was at the desk, talking to yet another librarian, a man this time. Then he signed a form and came over with another book. It was a history of Mumbles.

'Why, for heaven's sake?' she asked.

'I wanted to know why it's called Mumbles. You don't know, do you?'

'No,' she said, never having thought about it.

'The librarian said I should look it up myself. He probably doesn't know either. That's what my teachers always say when they don't know something, "Look it up yourself, boy, it's the only way to learn!"'

'I'd have thought we had enough things to look up,' said Cerian, but without conviction. Now she *had* thought about it, why *was* Mumbles called Mumbles?

Dylan started leafing through the book. Cerian shrugged and went back to the directories.

'Listen to this!' hissed Dylan. 'It says Mumbles had the oldest passenger railway in the world. They called it the Mumbles Express and it did six miles an hour. I go much faster than that on my bike.'

'You wouldn't like to help with this, would you?' asked Cerian.

'In a minute . . . Did you know everyone in Mumbles used to eat oysters all the time? But then they overfished and there weren't enough oysters left and people were pratically starving—they had to open soup kitchens. What's a soup kitchen?'

'Like my house,' said Cerian.

'Hey, if there are oysters there must be pearls! It says there are oyster shells all over the beach.'

'*I've* never seen any pearls,' said Cerian dubiously.

A man at the next table was glaring at them. Dylan lapsed into silence. Then he began to giggle.

'What is it?' asked Cerian.

'Why Mumbles is called that—the name comes from the "two protuberant rocky islets . . . "'

'I know that.'

'Yes, but the name comes from a Danish word *marmles* which means *breasts*. Fancing calling a place after a pair of boobs!'

'I don't believe it,' said Cerian, pushing him aside. 'Look, it says it might be from the Welsh . . . '

At lunchtime they went in search of food and found a café selling hot pasties. 'I'm not really hungry,' said Dylan, looking at the price.

'Oh.' Cerian bought her pasty and munched it walking down the road. 'You want some? It's a bit big for me.'

'Okay.'

' . . . Actually,' she said a little later, 'I'm still hungry. Maybe I'd better get another one after all.'

So they went back to the shop and shared a second pasty.

'Thanks,' said Dylan.

'You're welcome.'

They walked on down to the marina. The harbour basin was full of sailing dinghies and speedboats and cabin cruisers, all white and sparkling.

'There's people live on that one,' said Cerian, pointing to a big cruiser.

Dylan was impressed. Wouldn't it be great to live on a boat, go where you wanted.

There was the sound of a flute playing. Sitting with his bare feet dangling over the water was a young man wearing patched jeans, holed T-shirt and a hat with a feather in it. Lying to one side was a rucksack and on the other a scruffy dog. Behind him was a cap with a few coins in it. A woman

29

tossed some money into it but he took no notice, just carried on playing.

Dylan wondered if he could learn to play the flute. It would be great to live like that, do as he pleased, wander where he willed with a dog at his heels. He pushed out of his mind the memory of the miserable faces he used to see huddled in doorways in London, black with dirt and blue with cold, and stinking.

'I'll buy you an ice cream if you like,' said Cerian, breaking in on his thoughts. He couldn't resist but, crunching his cornet, had a twinge of conscience.

'Cerian . . . What—I mean, do your parents mind about me eating at your house all the time?'

'Oh no. There's always plenty to eat. Anyway, they don't bother about things like that.'

'They're not much like other people's parents, are they?'

'I don't think it's that,' said Cerian. 'I think they're just more honest. Ordinary parents pretend to be interested in rules and how you ought to behave and that because they think it's good for you. My parents don't pretend.'

'I've done a stew for supper,' said Tom, 'for a change.'

The only difference from the usual soup seemed to be that there was less liquid and the vegetables came in larger lumps. Cerian caught Dylan's eye and grinned.

'Match tomorrow,' said Tom. 'Want to come along, Dylan?'

'What sort of match?'

'Mini-rugby,' explained Cerian. 'Dad's the coach.'

'Funny time of year for rugby, isn't it?'

'This is special,' explained Tom. 'Grudge match.'

'It'll be good,' said Cerian. 'And it's Sunday tomorrow so the library will be shut anyway.'

'What are you two doing all this time at the library?'

'Local history research,' said Cerian blandly. 'Do you know why Mumbles is called Mumbles?'

'No,' said Tom.
'No,' said Bea. 'Why is it?'
'Well,' said Cerian . . .

CHAPTER FIVE
Sunday 21 July

Next morning Dylan sat eating porridge while Tom
panicked and Cerian looked for her father's kit, fed the dog,
fed the cat, found Tom's notes and answered the telephone,
which rang what seemed like thirty-three times with
messages about the match. Bea was still in bed, catching up
on lost sleep.

The rain had cleared overnight: it was a radiantly sunny
day. Barkis, asleep under the kitchen table, refused to be
moved.

There was a forty-minute drive up the valley to the
ground at Pontypandy. Dylan having unwisely revealed
that he had never played rugby, Tom spent the journey
explaining the rules. By the time they arrived, Dylan was
totally confused.

Tom parked the van and was instantly engulfed by a tide
of small boys in red shirts.

'Have we come to watch a load of little kids?' demanded
Dylan.

'Sure,' said Cerian. 'I told you, mini-rugby.'

'I thought that meant it wouldn't last so long.' Dylan was
now in a really bad mood.

'Don't you like sport?'

'I like football.'

'I thought you wanted to be Welsh? Anyway, this is
different. We're playing Bennington.'

'So?'

'So they're big rivals. Everyone goes berserk. And they
haven't played for ages because the season hasn't started
yet.'

While waiting for the match to start, they sat and drank
Coke in the clubhouse, which smelt of beer, cigarettes and

sweat. The walls were lined with team photographs and there were endless cabinets of silver cups.

A coach drew up outside, hooting. Out tumbled a flood of small children, followed, not much more sedately, by the grown-ups. Despite the heat they wore club scarves, some even club hats. They piled into the bar, all trying to buy drinks at once, exchanging greetings and insults with the Pontypandy supporters.

Cerian was talking—shouting, rather, over the din—with friends. I'm not staying here, thought Dylan, hating the noise and the smoke and the smell. He squeezed out and went to lie on the grass. The sky was blue and there was a chaffinch singing. Chaffinch was one he could tell just by the song; he remembered his mother telling him to listen how each phrase ended with 'Shakespeare'. *Not* his mother.

'You'll get trampled on if you lie there,' said Cerian. 'Come on, our side's over there.'

Tom looked enormous surrounded by a crowd of very small boys. One was sucking his thumb.

'The under-eights,' explained Cerian. 'They play first. Then the *real* match, the under-tens.'

'Where's Bennington?' he asked.

Cerian looked vague. 'Gloucestershire, somewhere, I think. England, anyway.'

Eventually the maelstrom sorted itself out, Pontypandy in red, Bennington in blue, the referee towering over the players as he supervised the toss. Tom on the touchline was still shouting advice and encouragement. As the game started, suddenly everyone else was shouting as well. Very small boys ran around with the ball, panicked and ran in the opposite direction, fell over and jumped on each other to a crescendo of shrieks from the supporters.

'Come on, Ponty! Come on, Bennington! *Go for it! GET HIM!*'

Dylan stared in astonishment at so many respectable-looking parents leaping, screaming, beside themselves.

The players were getting muddier. One of the Benning-ton side, a ginger-haired boy, always seemed to be at the

33

bottom of the heap. As the whistle blew for half-time, he was led away in tears.

Clean substitutes were sent on and the teams changed ends to howls of abuse from their respective coaches.

Then Bennington scored.

The English parents cheered wildly. Pontypandy booed. Tom was transformed, no longer genial and jolly. He looked, thought Dylan, as if he was going to explode.

But it was the only try of the match. When the whistle blew the boys tottered from the field.

'*RIGHT!*' yelled Tom at the under-10s. 'You lot will bloody well have to show them!'

Pale, teeth clenched, the Pontypandy team trickled on to the pitch to the accompaniment of jeers from the English. Then came the Bennington team, bunched up round one, taller and broader than the rest, who was swaggering with a smile of anticipated triumph. With a shock Dylan realized it was a girl.

'That's Melanie,' said Cerian. 'She's really bad news.'

Bennington won the toss and at first seemed to be having all their own way, heaving and battering ever closer to the Pontypandy end. Melanie seemed to have the ball most of the time. She had a technique all her own: rather than trying to dodge the opposition, she simply marched over them. She was slow but unstoppable.

With three of the Pontypandy boys desperately clinging to bits of her, she waded over the line to score the first try. A fair-haired boy kicked the conversion.

Tom was almost in tears. He ran on to the pitch, called his team together, whispered urgently to them.

Whatever he had said seemed to work. Suddenly the Welsh side had the ball. Melanie had inexplicably fallen over. Pontypandy scored.

The supporters erupted. Cheers from the Welsh, cries of 'Foul!' from the English.

The referee ignored them.

The game surged this way and that, then Dylan and Cerian had to leap back out of the way as a scrum developed right by them. To and fro it heaved, then a boy screamed and Melanie was out of the scrum, ball clutched to her chest, ploughing through the opposition. 'She bit me!' screamed the boy, holding out his arm.

Tom looked. 'Bloody hell!' he cried. 'Teethmarks! *Foul!*'

The referee blew his whistle.

Tom charged across the pitch, dragging the injured boy, straight at the English lines. The Welsh parents followed. Tom was yelling, the Bennington people shouted back. Then someone threw a punch. Then chaos.

The referee abandoned his whistle and joined in.

The drive home passed in silence. Tom, with a black eye, his clothes spattered from someone's nose-bleed, looked thoughtful.

'I think,' said Cerian, watching her father fumble for the door key, 'I think he's wondering how to explain to Mum.'

'I'm off,' said Dylan. 'See you.'

Cerian sighed. It looked like being a difficult afternoon.

Dylan walked downhill, towards the sea. The tide was far out, the bay empty as far as Mumbles as if someone had pulled the plug out. All along the beach were heaped-up banks of shells.

There were lots of oyster-shells. Head down, Dylan hunted for pearls.

How much would a pearl be worth, he wondered. If he found enough for a necklace, that had to be a lot of money. Thousands, maybe. Hundreds at least. He might buy some stuff and mend the cowshed roof. Or . . .

He could do anything, go anywhere.

He didn't know where to go.

He wanted to go home. But he didn't have a home. First he'd been given away, like jumble. Then he'd been betrayed. They'd lied to him, pretended he was their kid, pretended he was someone called Simon, pretended he was English. They'd stolen his name, his identity. When he watched sport on the telly he always cheered for England.

He'd made jokes at school about the Welsh, stupid people who ate leeks all the time and sang on top of mountains and burned cottages and talked funny. There'd been a kid in Juniors come from Wales, they'd all jeered at him, 'Taffy was a Welshman, Taffy was a thief, Taffy came to my house And stole a leg of beef.' Then instead of being an English boy called Simon, he found he was a Welsh boy called Dylan. And all his life the people he had thought were his parents had been someone else, pretending they had the right to push him around and tell him off. It wasn't his fault things went wrong. They'd never really wanted him. He wasn't going to stay where he wasn't wanted. If that was what parents were like, he'd do without them.

Grown-ups were so hypocritical. Always claiming they knew best, and then look how they behaved. If he'd got into a fight he'd have been put on bread and water for a week.

There weren't any pearls.

Out on the mudflats the oystercatchers laughed at him.

As evening fell, Dylan walked back through the town, bought a bag of chips, ate half and chucked the rest away. He didn't feel like food.

He didn't feel like sleeping either. He sat on the wall by the cowshed watching the sun grow as it sank, splash into a flood of orange as it met the horizon, then spill away. The last birds of evening fell silent. An owl drifted overhead, noiseless, hunting.

The sky was full of bats. The air rang with their unheard cries.

Voices he couldn't hear were calling him. Reluctantly he picked his way over the rubble to the farmhouse door.

The moonlight trickled silver shards into the blackness.

Drawn despite himself, he walked through to the inner room.

A woman in an old-fashioned dress was crouched on a stool, leaning forward, pleading. She had a mane of fair hair, pale skin and dark eyes, burning. She was talking, calling, begging him to hear her.

But he could not. Her mouth opened and closed in silence.

Beyond, by the hearth, a small boy stood staring at him.

A man was stooped, stoking the fire. He was dressed in an old-fashioned way as well. He turned, poker in hand.

Dylan looked away, back at the woman. She seemed closer now, almost clutching at his jeans.

Her eyes burned into his. Through the blood drumming in his ears he thought he caught a word: help.

Was he to help her, or she him?

Suddenly he was aware of the man looming above her, the poker raised in his hand, his face contorted.

Dylan screamed.

The figures vanished. Only the moonlight remained in the empty house.

CHAPTER SIX

Monday 22 July

Dylan woke in the middle of the night. The ground was hard. He was cold.

He was miserable.

He couldn't get back to sleep. Eventually he crawled out of the sleeping-bag, wrapped it around his shoulders and walked to the top of the hill, trying to get warm.

From the top of the ridge he could see the lights of Swansea laid out in ordered rows. Everyone was sleeping there, proper families, each behind their own closed doors. Only he was awake, alone, with nowhere to go. Why me, he thought? It's not fair. What have *I* done?

For a while he thought, maybe I'll walk into town, find a police station, get them to take me home. But he knew he couldn't. That wasn't home. He wasn't theirs, and they didn't want him.

Coming to Swansea had been a mistake. He didn't want to find his real mother. She'd given him away before, she wouldn't want him now.

Nobody wanted him.

Why me, he thought again? I've never done anything.

It was then that Dylan, who used to be Simon, who had a mum and dad and lived an ordinary life, it was then that he had an idea. It was horrifying, it was exciting, it was impossible. But as he sat and watched the light grow in the sky, so the idea grew.

As the birds began to sing, he made up his mind.

Back down the fields the farmhouse stood in shadow still, whispering, calling to him. He turned his back on it, curled up in his sleeping-bag and, finally, slept.

It was nearly ten when he woke. Remembering, he panicked. In the full light of day things seem different. But then, he wasn't Simon any more. He was Dylan. He was free to do what he liked. He had nothing to lose. And he was hungry.

The bicycle was a real piece of luck. He saw it as he walked down through the housing estate, lying on a grass verge. A Peugeot mountain bike, ten gears. His friend Neil had one last birthday. Nearly £200 it had been. Just lying there on the grass.

He was on it and pedalling away down the hill and no one had noticed.

Dylan parked the bike outside the Spar. He picked up a basket as he went in. He put a small loaf of bread in it, then walked over to the drinks shelves. The can of Coke went inside his jacket, nestled at his waist. He spent some time choosing the cheese. A large pack of Stilton. Money no object. It joined the Coke. A bar of chocolate followed it. He added a packet of crisps to the bread, then queued up to pay for the contents of the basket. His heart was thumping. But the cashier didn't even look up as she took the money for the bread and crisps. He dropped his change in his pocket and sauntered from the shop, packed his trophies into the saddle-bag and swung his leg over the bike. He risked a glance behind; no one was taking any notice, no one rushing from the shop, fist waving. It had been too easy, he felt, as he cycled off downhill. Like trying to break a door down and finding it was open.

He followed the route Tom had taken in the van, westwards towards Gower. He didn't know anywhere else to go. But within a mile or two he lost his way. Perhaps he should have stolen a map as well.

Gradually, the narrow streets gave way to country lanes. He turned left and right almost at random, although the wind in his face told him when he was heading west.

It was when his stomach growled hungrily that he saw the dead-end lane which must lead down to the sea. He turned down it between hedges high with unripe blackberries.

39

The lane finished in a tiny car-park overlooking the sea. A footpath led away, down the cliff. But he didn't like to leave the bike in case someone pinched it. He perched on a wall and laid out his picnic. The bread was too fresh to slice properly with only a penknife; he tore lumps from the loaf and wrapped them around slivers of cheese. The Coke, shaken during the ride, spurted over his jeans.

As he lifted the can to his lips he heard an engine. A red Sierra turned into the car-park, spattering the gravel. A small boy jumped out, shouting, 'I can see the se-e-e-e-a.' A man and a woman followed. They took no notice of Dylan watching from the wall as they unloaded rucksack, coolbox and bucket and spade. The woman called to the boy, who was being an aeroplane: 'Come on, love.' She held the coolbox in her right hand, stretched out the other to the boy. He clutched it and seized his father's free right hand. Together the three moved off down the path, the boy swinging from their hands, shouting, 'Wheeeeee.'

Dylan's throat contracted, remembering when he had swung in just the same way, flying through the air in his parents' hands. He watched them out of sight.

The woman had left her handbag in the car, on the front seat. That was stupid. You should always lock valuables in the boot. Leaving it in full view like that was asking for trouble. Anyone could take it.

There was no one around, no sounds except a crow cawing and the distant hiss of the sea.

There were plenty of stones.

He chose a large pointed stone, clutched it like a club, swung it at the car window. The glass collapsed in a shower of fragments. Shocked at the noise, he reached in, grabbed the bag, ran for his bike and was away, heart pounding.

He was frightened a car would come, someone would see him with the handbag. He pedalled at top speed, hurtling round the bends. Suddenly there *was* a car, rushing towards him. He panicked, swerved violently, there was a screech of brakes and the car slammed into the hedge. He shot past and away, shaking so that he could hardly control the bike, but too terrified to stop.

Dylan was miles away and completely lost before he pushed the bike through a gate and collapsed in a field. Gradually, his heart stilled. In the distance, the drone of a tractor. He lay on his back watching high-level jets make scratch marks on the sky.

Then he emptied the bag out on to the grass. There was a purse, make-up bag, diary, comb and a small pack of tissues. The purse contained £59.33, library tickets, driving licence, a hospital appointment card and a photograph of the little boy.

There was a robin singing in the hedge.

He stuffed the money into his back pocket, put everything else back in the bag and hung it in a hawthorn bush. Then he got back on the bike and headed off slowly in what he hoped was the direction of Swansea. Missing its weight at his belt he realized he'd left his penknife and the remains of the bread and cheese in the car-park. Still, he could buy new. He had loads of money now.

He felt sick.

Much to Cerian's relief, her parents were back to normal the morning after the rugby match. Nobody mentioned the *Western Mail*, in which 'Scuffle at Mini-Rugby Clash' had made page five. Tom, with that absent expression which meant he was plotting a new gnome murder, retired to his studio.

Cerian washed up the breakfast things, then sat down with a book while waiting for Dylan. The book was supposed to be a mystery but was, she thought, a lot less interesting than looking for Dylan's mother.

At half past ten he still hadn't turned up. She decided to go and look for him.

He wasn't there. His sleeping-bag lay in a tumbled heap surrounded by empty crisp packets, but that was all.

Cerian wandered around, looked into the pigsty, then, reluctantly, into the house. There was no one there. Only the birds. For a while she sat on a wall, waiting. But she felt she was wasting her time. There was a very empty feeling to the place.

She left in the direction of the library. Dylan hadn't been much use hunting through the electoral registers. She might as well do it on her own. She smiled, imagining how casually she would say, 'Oh, by the way, I've found your mother', how pleased he would be. It would be worth a bit of effort.

Bea was working at home that morning. She had masses of paperwork to catch up with, and it should be quieter away from the office. Yawning, she emptied her briefcase out on to the table. It had been a hectic weekend, she'd been called out both nights—twice on Saturday. Why, she wondered, couldn't people have their crises between nine and five, Monday to Friday? Sitting down to the heaps of files, she sighed. Not for the first time she wished she had never become a social worker.

The St Bernard slumped by her side. He had had a trying morning, sorting out the postman.

Bea made a start on yesterday's mail.

For a few minutes silence reigned, broken only by the sound of pages turning and the dog's steady snore.

Bea slit open the next envelope. '*Simon Wells . . . age 13 . . . missing from home . . . may be in Swansea area.*' The photograph of a boy in school uniform was very blurred but seemed vaguely familiar.

The telephone rang. Bea went out into the hall to answer it. Mulligan walked in, sniffed at Barkis, then jumped up on to the table, looking for somewhere comfortable. She curled up on the photograph and started to wash.

Bea came back into the room and picked up the next envelope.

Mulligan slept.

It was late afternoon before Dylan got back to Swansea. He bought a bicycle lock and secured the bike to a lamp-post. Then he bought a Swiss army knife with thirteen different blades and, with that hooked to his jeans, felt better. He had fish and chips, then went to the cinema.

It was an American cops film, and pretty stupid. He tried to take the crooks' side, but they were really dumb. They all got shot or put in jail. And the detectives were awful fat slobs. Why didn't they make films where the baddies won?

Dylan woke, running from a dream, hearing again the dull slam of the car into the hedge and the shower of glass from the broken window. He felt worse than he'd ever done. He couldn't even give the money back; he needed it and anyway he'd spent some.

A dog was howling somewhere in the distance, a low, monotonous, hopeless wailing.

Dylan lay and wished he was dead. Finally the dog fell quiet.

And then he heard singing.

It was a woman's voice; a quiet, happy tune, with frequent pauses as if she were singing while she worked.

Dylan wasn't sure if he could really hear the voice or if it was inside his head. Who could be singing here in the middle of the night?

Gradually the blackness in his head began to lighten. The song beckoned. He got up, pulled on his shoes, and went out into the dark.

The farmhouse was full of light. Dylan stopped on the threshold. Behind him he was aware of the thick black night, the piled-up bricks, the brambles clutching his clothes. But before him the house was intact, ceilings and staircase undamaged, the floor swept clean, and glass in the windows which drenched the room with sunlight. The woman was there, but this time she didn't seem to see him. She was painting a wall blue, and singing. The sun shone in her long fair hair.

Dylan felt in the pocket of his jeans, where he had put the

43

piece of blue painted plaster. It was still there. His hand closed over it.

The woman sang as she worked.

When she had finished she tidied up, then put the little table back by the newly-painted wall, and on it put a jug of daffodils, yellow against the blue and lit by the sunshine that streamed through the open door.

Dylan felt someone coming. A man came in, walking right by him, not noticing, as if he wasn't there. The woman turned to greet the man, smiling.

He didn't respond. He put a sack down in the doorway, heaved his boots off, then sank into his chair with a deep sigh. The woman brought him a mug of cider which he took with a grunt and swallowed down, eyes closed. 'Lunch is nearly ready,' she said.

At that he opened his eyes. 'Then be quick about it, Beth. I've no time to waste sitting around here.'

The woman dropped more wood into the range, sliced some bread.

It was not until the man had mopped up the last of his soup that he looked up and noticed the wall.

'Do you like it?' Beth asked, leaning forward.

'Where did you get the paint?'

She flushed. 'It was Mr Bullen gave it me, he had it spare.'

Suddenly he was shouting. 'Spare, was it? I'm not having charity, do you hear? We may not have much, but by God I'll work for what we have! I'll not take charity from the likes of him!'

The woman sat with her head bowed. The man was striding up and down the room, his right fist pounding the palm of his left hand, complaining about the paint and that she frittered her time picking daffodils while he was working all hours and what was she doing talking to Bullen and they so little to live on and the baby coming . . . Finally he stopped. He stood looking down at her, his breath coming in short gasps. She sat still, staring at the table.

'I'm sorry, Geraint. I wanted to please you.'

He sighed and turned away. He picked up the sack which he had left lying by the door and dropped it in her lap. 'Here,' he said, 'busy yourself with this. Since you have all this time to spare.'

And then he walked through the doorway where Dylan stood and was gone.

Beth opened the sack and took out a tiny pink piglet.

CHAPTER SEVEN

Tuesday 23 July

Dylan opened his eyes, shook his head, trying to clear it. Inside his head he could still see them, Beth and Geraint, but they weren't there. It might have been a dream, except that he was huddled by the doorway of the farmhouse, not wrapped in his sleeping-bag in the cowshed.

The sun was shining, as it had been in the middle of the night. But the farmhouse was derelict once more.

He closed his eyes again. He could feel them there, feel Beth's confusion, feel Geraint's pain as he shouted, feel the piglet's warmth as Beth stretched her hand into the sack.

They were, he supposed, ghosts; but they seemed more real than people, as if he had been, by turns, first Beth, then Geraint, then Beth again.

He thought of going to tell Cerian about it, but decided not to. She wouldn't understand, might even laugh. And anyway it was his, for him alone.

Then the other memories came flooding back, the things he'd rather forget.

Maybe he'd take the bike back. That was one thing he could do. The idea cheered him up.

He dragged it out from behind the hedge where he had hidden it and wheeled it up across the fields. It was a good bike, but it had got him into trouble. He'd be glad to be rid of it. And the boy who owned it would be glad to have it back.

Riding through the housing estate he started to worry. What if someone saw him put it back? Perhaps he'd better wait till after dark.

Too late. A shout. 'Hey! You! That's my bike!' Dylan turned, saw a group of boys, one in a red T-shirt, yelling. He wobbled across the road, crashed into the verge, jumped off the bike and ran. Stones flew around him; one hit him on the back of the head. Dizzy, he lurched on, feeling a hot stickiness on his neck. Any moment he expected the boy to come after him on the bike.

He turned left, pelted down the street which turned suddenly into a dead end. With scarcely a pause he went up and over the wooden fence at the end and found himself in a garden.

A small girl in a summer dress was laying out a dolls' tea-set on the lawn. She stopped and stared at him.

He halted, panting, then began to sidle past. Suddenly, she started screaming. He took to his heels, catching a brief glimpse of a woman coming out of the back door as he fled up the side passage.

Half running, half walking, his head spinning, he went on, never stopping till he found himself in a park, all ordered flower-beds and close-mown grass. And a drinking fountain. He gulped at the water, splashed it on his face, then slumped down in the shade of a tree. He didn't dare touch the back of his head, where he could feel the blood still trickling.

It was evening before Dylan moved. He felt muzzy, and a bit sick, and not at all hungry, although he hadn't eaten since the fish and chips the previous day.

He took a long way round to avoid the housing estate and headed for what he now thought of as home.

This time he went straight to the farmhouse, his hand in his pocket clenched around the piece of painted wall-plaster.

The woman—Beth—was filling a bottle with milk. The piglet had grown. 'Outside,' said Beth, as he grunted and prodded at her skirt. She led the way out and settled herself down, laughing as the piglet knocked at her hands in his eagerness to get at the bottle.

He gulped noisily at the milk, tail wagging.

When all the milk was gone, the piglet relinquished the teat with a sigh and waited hopefully for signs of another bottle. None came. He subsided to the ground, his head in Beth's lap.

Her fingers moved gently among the sparse hairs on his leathery back.

Beth reached out to the daisies that spangled the grass and began weaving them into a chain. The piglet snorted in his sleep. The daisy-chain grew longer.

She joined the ends of the chain, then tickled the piglet behind the ears. He woke, blinking, and raised his snout. She put the daisy-chain round his broad neck, laughing.

'And what do you think you're at?'

It was Geraint, scowling.

Beth scrambled to her feet. 'I'm sorry. I was just having a rest. I was tired, Geraint.'

He turned his back on her and strode into the house. 'Tired, is it? *I'm* tired. And while I'm working, you're making daisy-chains for pigs!'

'I'm sorry,' she said again. 'It's the baby makes me weary. The midwife said I should rest.'

'I suppose that's my fault!'

'Don't be angry,' said Beth. 'I'll get your meal now.'

He threw himself down in his chair. But almost at once he slumped into a doze.

Beth laid the food on the table, tiptoeing around the room. When the meal was ready she crossed over to his chair, looking down at him. His eyes were watering and his face grey. When he began to stir, she leant down and kissed his forehead.

His eyes still shut, he reached out a hand and pulled her down on to his knee, holding her close.

'Come and eat,' she said. 'You'll feel better then.'

He smiled. 'I don't think I've the strength to open my eyes.'

They sat still.

At last Beth said, 'Come, the food will spoil.' She stood up.

'Aye.' He stretched, rose to his feet.

The man ate quickly. He mopped his plate with some bread then asked for the cheese.

'Geraint, I'm sorry, there isn't any. You finished it yesterday.'

'Then why didn't you make fresh?'

'There wasn't any milk,' she faltered.

'And why wasn't there any milk?'

She was silent.

'That pig's had it, hasn't it?' said Geraint. '*Hasn't it?*'

She nodded.

'Well, it won't have any more! That animal's for us to eat, not for it to eat our food! I'll take it to market tomorrow.'

'It's all right,' said Beth quickly. 'He's ready to wean now, really he is; I won't give him any more milk. Please, Geraint. He's too young to take to market.'

The piglet, brought by the shouting, trotted up, grunting.

For a moment Geraint glared at her, then, muttering, 'To hell with it', threw down his knife and crashed off upstairs.

Silence fell. Beth, cuddling the piglet, rocked to and fro, eyes closed.

CHAPTER EIGHT

Wednesday 24 July

Next morning, Dylan went round to Cerian's house. Odd as they were, at least it was somewhere to go.

There was no reply. He rang three times and was just about to give up when a voice spoke behind him, making him jump. It was Mamgu, carrying a shopping basket. 'She's out. And Bea's at work and Tom's potting.'

'Oh.' Dylan didn't know what to do.

'You can come in and talk to me if you like.'

'All right.' Realizing he'd sounded rude, he added, 'Thank you.'

'You look down in the dumps, lad,' she said as she let him into her flat. 'I'll make some tea. Are you hungry?'

Dylan nodded.

'Could do with a bath as well, couldn't you? Bathroom's over there; there's a clean towel in the airing cupboard; don't leave the bath dirty. And—here—I've been collecting for a jumble sale. Have a look through and see if you can find something to fit. It's all clean.' She handed him two bulging carrier bags.

Bemused, Dylan did as he was told. The bath was on two levels; like a seat at one end, with handles to make it easy to get out of. It was impossible to lie down for a good soak, but the water was hot and comforting. He would have liked to wash his hair, but decided he'd better not, in case the cut on his head started bleeding again. But at least he could wipe away the hard crust of dried blood on his neck and down his back.

He mopped the bath out afterwards, even used cleaner. Then he tipped the jumble out on the floor, found a pair of cord jeans and a sweatshirt which looked all right. There wasn't any underwear but he wouldn't have fancied that anyway, not knowing where it had come from. He washed his underpants in the sink, rubbed them on a towel and put them back on. They were nylon and would soon dry. He finished dressing and went back into the sitting-room feeling warm and tingly.

There was a wonderful smell of bacon.

'I can always manage two breakfasts,' said Mamgu. 'Will you help with the tray, please?'

There were two plates heaped high with bacon, eggs, mushrooms and tomatoes, a loaf of soft white bread, butter, marmalade and a large pot of tea.

'All that vegetarian stuff they give you downstairs,' said Mamgu, picking up her knife and fork. 'You must be starving.'

They ate in a contented silence.

'Do you want to tell me?'

Dylan looked up, realizing that she must have guessed most of it and there wasn't any point in lying to her.

So he told her about the rows at home and about running away and looking for his real mother, only now he didn't want to find her.

She listened without saying anything, just nodding encouragement.

And when he'd finished, she didn't ask silly questions like, 'What are you going to do?'

Instead she asked if he'd pass the marmalade.

Then she said, 'Dylan Thomas was brought up in Swansea.'

'Who was he?'

'My poor child! Not to know Dylan Thomas! These English schools . . . He was the greatest poet of the twentieth century. Had a terrible reputation when he was alive, they said he was always drinking; there's hardly a pub in Swansea he's not supposed to have visited. Just up the road he lived as a child, by Cwmdonkin Park. I think he upset a lot of people. They've forgiven him now, though, put up a statue to him. Do you like poetry?'

'Ye-es. It depends. I don't like soppy stuff. We had to do Sir Walter Scott last term.'

'That's not poetry. That's doggerel. I mean *real* poetry, poetry that sings to your soul. And you named Dylan!'

'Do you think I'm named after him?' he asked.

'I think you might be. Would you like that?'

'I don't know. Maybe.'

She looked at the clock. 'I have to go out now. Would you like to come?'

'Where to?'

'Up the Swansea valley. The village where I was born.'

'Okay.'

'Then if you'll just carry the dishes through to the kitchen for me, I'll do the washing-up later. It's a bore, washing-up, isn't it?'

They took Tom's van. Once out of Swansea, the road spread itself and headed for the hills.

After half an hour or so, they threaded their way along a zigzag village street, turned down a potholed track and parked outside a big low building.

Mamgu pulled on the handbrake with a grunt of relief. 'This was the pithead baths,' she said. 'The miners didn't want them built. They didn't believe in washing their backs, only at weekends: they thought washing would weaken them. They'd have this black square on their backs. My father used to wear—you wouldn't know what they were like—he wore these wool vests with sleeves so as not to dirty the bedclothes. And the miners' wives didn't want the baths either, they thought their men would catch cold having to shower, then go out in the cold and the rain.' She laughed. 'The owners rigged the ballot and built the baths anyway.'

'Did everyone work in the mine then?' asked Dylan.

'Almost. There'd be hundreds of men every shift. When they came up from the pit they'd strip off their dirty clothes and put them in the dirty clothes lockers ready for next day, then they'd go through the shower room and then into the room with the clean clothes lockers. Then they'd light up their cigarettes and walk down the road together.'

'Were there accidents?'

'Of course. Not what you're probably thinking of, no great disasters. But men got killed in the pit, or died of the coughing, after. But it wasn't all bad, the men brought home good money and the Miners' Welfare built a cinema and a snooker parlour and a hall for meetings.

'When the pits closed the heart went out of the place. People went home and shut their doors. Now it's all commuters driving down to Neath and Swansea. Not like it was when I was a girl.' She fell silent.

'When did you leave?'

'More than forty years ago. I was lucky, got the best man in the village, the one with brains. He got a job as a teacher in Swansea. Didn't earn as much as the miners, of course, but we thought we were really grand.' She smiled at some inward memory, then sighed.

'This place now—they had money from the Welsh Office and workers on a government training scheme to do it up and now it's a concert hall and a sports hall and multi-gym and sauna and solarium. But they can't get the people to come and use it. Strange, isn't it, the village didn't want it in the first place and it still doesn't. Anyway, come on in, I have to meet some friends and they do a very good lunch here for a pound. Don't worry, I'll treat you!'

It was a good lunch: onion soup, sausages beans and chips, strawberry crumble and custard. Neither had any difficulty eating it, despite their late breakfast. Afterwards Mamgu settled down with her friends and a pot of tea, and Dylan was given free run of the multi-gym. He tried out the rowing machine, the cycle, the thing for running on the spot, and all the weight-lifting apparatus. Then he lay down on the out-of-order sun-bed and fell fast asleep.

When he woke up it was time for tea and cakes.

They took a long way home, driving up the valley first, past square-topped hills, uniformly green, the relics of past mining.

'And that's what mining's like now,' said Mamgu as they came round a bend. She pulled over on to the verge and turned off the engine.

The whole hillside had been gouged out, with huge machines—cranes and excavators—seeming tiny in the bottom of the hole.

'Open-cast. They don't dig pits any more, they dig out the whole mountain.' She shook her head. 'They always say they'll put things back again afterwards, but you can't, not to make them the same as they used to be. Still, they say the nation needs the coal. We don't get much chance to argue. The local councils were all against allowing open-cast mining, but the government overruled them. It's just the way it's always been, Wales gives and England takes.'

'Are you a Wesh nationalist?'

'Don't sound so shocked. You're Welsh too, aren't you?'

'I dunno. I mean, yes, I suppose I'm Welsh, but I don't know what it means. Like Welsh people don't seem to talk Welsh much or—or be any different really.'

'You're right, of course. There's not many speak Welsh round Swansea now, not like when I was a girl. I grew up speaking Welsh but Tom never learned it, or only a few words. My fault. No, you can buy the same clothes and eat the same food from the same cafés and watch the same television programmes in Swansea or Birmingham or London or Glasgow. But there is still something different about being Welsh. I think it's something to do with a sense of place, of feeling you belong to a place . . .'

'I don't,' said Dylan. 'I don't belong anywhere.'

'Oh, but you do. Though maybe you've still got to find out where.'

They sat in silence, watching as the machinery pecked away at the mountain.

CHAPTER NINE
Thursday 25 July

Cerian picked her way up the library steps through a crowd
of girls clustered round the *No Loitering* sign. They were
talking about boys. Cerian felt both awkward, not belong-
ing, and superior.

She collected the electoral registers and settled down at
her usual table. The sounds and smells of the reference
library were familiar and comfortable now, and the task of
methodically working through the registers reassuringly
straightforward. At home she never knew what to expect
next: here there were no such problems.

So, when after half an hour or so of quiet turning of
pages, she came across Catherine Elizabeth Hughes, she felt
almost cheated. She stared at the entry, sure it must be
wrong somewhere.

But there it was, Catherine Elizabeth Hughes, who was
living with Gavin Patrick Hughes at 94 Sebastopol
Terrace.

The telephone rang. The librarian answered it, laid the
receiver down on the desk, consulted a catalogue, fetched a
book from the stacks, leafed through the pages, finally
spoke down the telephone again.

Cerian was still gazing at the same entry. Looking for
Catherine Elizabeth was one thing, finding her another. If
she had an address then she was a real person. How did you
go about calling on a complete stranger and saying to her,
'I've come from your son who you gave away when he was a
baby?'

Then, with a great wave of relief, Cerian realized that this
might not be the *right* Catherine Elizabeth. Just because
there was this one didn't mean that there weren't others.

She would have to work right through the registers, right to the end, to make sure.

Thankfully she went back to work.

But after lunch was even more unsettling. For a start, someone had taken her place and she had to sit at the big table in the middle.

Then she found another Catherine Elizabeth, in Albemarle Road.

If there were two there might be lots.

How could she possibly tell which was the right one? Even worse than knocking on a stranger's door to say your son sent me would be if it was the wrong stranger.

There seemed to be a lot of coming and going in the library that afternoon. Cerian found it more and more difficult to keep to her system. Other unwelcome thoughts arose: what if the right Catherine Elizabeth had moved away?

What if she hasn't, Cerian told herself firmly, dragging her attention back to her list.

Or what if she's not on the telephone?

A short, fat man lowered himself into the chair opposite, hitting the seat with an audible thud and a smell of stale tobacco. Then he stood up again, took off his raincoat, folded it into a pile which he laid on the desk not far from Cerian's nose, thumped back into the chair and began to read the *Evening Post*. He was very noisy: the pages rustled, his breath wheezed and his clothes creaked.

Cerian found herself reading the newspaper upside down.

At the top of page four was a headline: 'HAVE YOU SEEN THIS BOY?' Underneath was a photo of Dylan.

They had the *Evening Post* delivered at home. It usually came around four. Cerian looked at her watch. Three fifty-five.

She had packed up, returned the registers and was out of the library in rather less than a minute.

It was twenty to five when, breathless, she burst in through the front door. The paper wasn't on the mat.

Was she too late? Was her father already reading it? Or had it not been delivered yet?

No sign of her father—or the paper—in the kitchen. She tiptoed through to the studio. Tom was hunched over a turntable, working the fine detail on a new gnome original. Cerian began to slip out again.

The door creaked.

Tom look up. 'Hello, what's the time?'

'Quarter to five.'

He laid down the modelling tool, stretched, easing his aching shoulders, groaned. 'Time I stopped. What do you think? Coming on, isn't he? A good victim.'

'Mmm,' said Cerian, relaxing. The paper hadn't come yet. 'He looks very smug.'

'That's the idea,' said Tom. 'The sort everyone loves to hate.' He began to wrap the model up in polythene. 'Put the kettle on, will you, love?'

Plugging in the kettle, Cerian let a wave of relief wash over her. All she had to do now was to keep an ear out for the clatter of the letter-box and make sure she got there first.

Tom sank down in the armchair, grunting his thanks for the cup of tea Cerian put by his side. He yawned and closed his eyes.

Then he opened them again. 'Has the paper come?'

'Not yet.' Cerian was leaning nonchalantly in the doorway.

'Sit down,' said Tom. 'You make the place look untidy.'

She perched on the chair nearest the door.

'What have you been doing with yourself, then?' Her father must be in one of his rare 'should take an interest in my daughter' phases.

'I went to the library.'

'Again? What do you do there?'

'Oh—um . . . ' She was saved having to answer. Barkis waddled in, carrying the *Evening Post*.

'Good boy!' said Tom. 'Thank you.' He took the paper and leafed through to the sports pages.

'There was ever such a funny man in the library,' she said.

'Mmm?' He turned a page, obviously not listening.

'I've decided what I'm going to be when I grow up,' she said desperately.

'Mmm?'

'I'm going to be a private detective.'

'Good idea.' He finished the sports section and went back to the front page.

The telephone rang. 'See who that is, will you?' asked Tom, turning to page two.

Cerian shot out to the hall. It was a wrong number.

'It's for you,' she said, fingers crossed behind her back.

Tom groaned, dropped the paper on the floor and went out.

Cerian pounced on the paper and fled upstairs to her room. Leaning against the closed door she turned to page four and began to read. *'Thirteen-year-old Simon Wells has been missing from his London home since last Monday . . . worried parents . . . found a letter . . . believe he may have come to Swansea . . .'*

'Cerian!'

She stuffed the paper under her mattress and went downstairs. 'Yes?'

'Who was it on the phone?' asked Tom.

'I don't know. A man.'

'What did you say to him? He'd rung off by the time I got there.'

'I just said I'd fetch you.'

'Oh well. I suppose he'll ring back, whoever it was.'

He sat down and began to drink his tea. 'It wasn't Bill, was it?'

'No. No one I know. He had a foreign accent,' added Cerian, elaborating.

'Not Japanese?' Tom asked, suddenly sitting up straight.

'No. Italian or Spanish or something.'

'I give up,' said Tom, shaking his head. Then: 'What happened to the paper?'

'Barkis ate it.'

'Did what?'

'Ate it. Well, not all of it, but it was so chewed I threw it away.'

'Why do I live in a madhouse?' complained Tom. 'Here.' He reached into his pocket and handed her a 50p piece. 'Go and get another one, will you? You can keep the change.'

Cerian walked down to the newsagents, turned round and walked back.

Tom was in the kitchen, making soup. She gave him back his 50p. 'Sold out,' she said.

'Bother. The one evening I fancy watching television, I don't know what's on. Stir this, will you, I'll ring Bea and ask her to get a paper.'

'Shall I do it for you?'

'No, I'll do it. You stir the soup.'

As he went out into the hall the doorbell rang. Barkis got up, growling. Tom fell over him. 'Horrible animal. You're a waste of space.'

Cerian concentrated on the soup, praying it wasn't the police at the door.

Dylan came in.

'Where have you been?' she asked.

'Around.' He sounded really fed up.

'Look, you'll have to be careful, there's a piece—' She broke off as Tom came back into the room.

'Well, lad, and what have you been up to?' asked Tom.

'Nothing,' said Dylan; but Cerian saw the look of alarm that flashed across his face.

Cerian was laying the table as Bea walked in, laden as usual. 'I remembered the paper,' she said proudly, dropping it on the table.

'Well done.' Tom turned from the cooker to give her a peck on the cheek.

With a speed worthy of a conjuror Cerian dropped the

paper behind the armchair and carried on arranging knives and spoons.

'Tea's ready,' said Tom.

Dylan had the feeling something was going on. He'd had a rotten day, wandering around not knowing what to do with himself.

The cat appeared beside him, looking hopeful. Dylan patted his lap, encouragingly. Mulligan jumped up, settled down, purred, claws extending and retracting through the knee of Dylan's jeans. Dylan winced, tried to stop the cat kneading.

Mulligan wriggled up on to the table underneath the cloth.

'Catch it!' roared Tom as a jug toppled.

Too late. The jug tipped over, sending a flood of apple juice over the slumbering Barkis.

The dog barked, deafeningly.

Cerian extracted the cat from beneath the cloth and went to fetch a mop.

'Can I have some more soup?' asked Bea, pulling a file out of her briefcase and starting to read.

'What happened to the paper?' asked Tom.

'I left it on the table,' said Bea.

'I haven't seen it,' said Cerian.

'I know where it is,' said Dylan helpfully. He fetched it from where it lay almost concealed behind the armchair, held it out to Tom.

'Good evening,' said Mamgu, coming in from the hall. 'Is that the evening paper?' She took it from Dylan, tucked it under her arm.

'I just wanted to see what was on television . . . ' said Tom.

'Let's play Scrabble,' said Cerian. 'We haven't had a game for ages.'

'Good idea,' said Mamgu. 'A very educational game.' As she headed for the door Cerian was almost sure she winked.

They all played Scrabble—Cerian and Dylan, Tom, Bea and Mamgu. Tom picked up almost nothing but vowels and hardly scored at all. Cerian couldn't concentrate. Dylan had most of the high scoring letters, q and x and z. But after dropping behind for a while Mamgu used all her letters at once to make 'criminal' and with fifty bonus points swept into a lead that no one else managed to catch.

It was dark by the time they finished, and Tom offered to see Dylan home.

'No, it's all right,' said Dylan. 'I'll manage.'

'I really think I should come with you,' said Tom. 'It's past ten.'

'No, it's okay, honest,' said Dylan.

'Leave him be,' said Mamgu. 'He can look after himself.'

'Well if you're sure . . . '

Cerian saw Dylan to the door. 'Your picture's in the paper,' she said. 'They're looking for you.'

Dylan went white.

'I managed to stop Mum and Dad seeing it,' she said, 'but Mamgu took the paper.'

Dylan was silent. How had the police got his picture? Would they send him to jail?

'Are you all right?' asked Cerian.

'Yes thanks,' he said mechanically. Then he shook himself, and said, 'See you.' But he didn't say when. He walked off into the dark.

'*No-o-o-o-o-o!*'

The sound ripped through the night. Dylan stumbled to his feet, ran, knowing through the confusion of broken sleep only that it was Beth screaming.

The afternoon sun shone in through the windows of the farmhouse.

Beth was sitting in a chair by the window, her dress stretched over the swell of her stomach. 'You're back early,' she said.

'Aye.' Geraint stripped off his jacket and waistcoat, rolled up his sleeves. 'I've come to slaughter the pig.'

Beth paled.

'I've sold half to Jones Post,' he went on. 'It's promised for tomorrow.'

'No,' she whispered.

'What do you mean, no?' Geraint looked up.

'You can't.'

'Can't what?'

'Kill him.'

'Of course I'm going to kill it. We've little enough to eat, you're not suggesting we should keep it eating its head off for ever, are you?'

'But he's . . . he's . . . ' Beth stopped. 'I reared him,' she said.

Geraint took her by the shoulders, looked down at her. 'Now, Beth, I told you not to get fond of that animal. It's a pig, and pigs are for eating.'

'But he's *different*. He's so clever, and so affectionate—'

'Beth, stop it. It's a pig, nothing but a pig. You mustn't take on. It's the baby coming gives you these fancies. You'll feel better when he's born.'

'Please, Geraint, not yet. At least not yet.' She was crying now.

He took a deep breath. 'The sooner the better. I'll get it over with. Go find something to occupy yourself with till it's done.'

He crossed to the hearth where the pig lay dozing. 'Come on, you.' He tweaked it by the ear and it stood up, blinking.

Beth slipped to the floor beside the pig, wrapped her arms around his neck. 'Don't do it, Geraint. Don't do it.'

He pulled her away, not roughly, took the pig by the ear and began to lead it out.

'No,' she said. 'No.' And then screamed, '*No-o-o-o-o-o!*'

Her hands were clasped over her ears, but Dylan heard the sudden outburst of squealing, as suddenly ended, the clatter of blood into the bucket, the crackle of fire.

Dylan stood among the ruins of the farmhouse, his nostrils full of the smell of pork fat and singeing hair.

CHAPTER TEN

Friday 26 July

The same smell was still in his nostrils when Dylan woke next morning in a shivering heap by the farmhouse door. It was raining.

He felt ill and confused. His head was muzzy, and he could not decide which part of his life was really happening.

His life in London seemed impossibly distant, as if it had happened to somebody else. His search for his mother felt like a fairy story, with no weight or substance. Stealing things, the police after him, was a nightmare. Only the unfolding dream, the haunting, whatever it was, felt real. Real, and urgent. But although he held the piece of painted plaster, turning it over and over in his hand, the farmhouse remained a ruin where weeds grew among the ashes.

The phone rang soon after breakfast. It was a man with a foreign accent. For a moment Cerian wondered if it was the same man who called yesterday, then she remembered she'd made him up. She went through to the pottery to fetch her father. 'Somebody on the phone for you. He sounds foreign.'

'Japanese?' asked Tom.

'Could be,' said Cerian cautiously.

Tom went to the phone at a run.

Cerian went upstairs to the attic. Mamgu was washing up. 'I came to see how you are,' said Cerian.

Mamgu cocked one eyebrow at her but said only, 'You can dry these if you like.'

Cerian, tea-towel in hand, roamed the kitchen, wandered casually into the sitting-room. There was no sign of yesterday's *Evening Post*, not even on the pile of papers that Mamgu kept for recycling.

The washing-up took some time, as Mamgu also saved bottles and cans to take to the Council's recycling skips.

'What are you going to do today?' asked Mamgu, scrubbing out a baked bean tin. 'The weather doesn't look too good.'

That was an understatement. It was pouring.

'Oh—I thought I might go to the library,' said Cerian.

'Is Dylan going with you?'

'No—just me.'

Mamgu nodded. 'You must be learning a lot,' she said. 'All this research. Perhaps I'll come with you.'

'Oh . . . ' Cerian couldn't think of an excuse.

'Perhaps I'd better not,' said Mamgu. 'I've rather a lot to do . . . '

Cerian fled before she could change her mind.

The library was quiet that morning. Cerian worked steadily. By half past twelve she had found a third Catherine Elizabeth Hughes and reached the end of her list of addresses.

She returned the registers thoughtfully. 'Finished, have you, dear? Did you find what you wanted?' asked the librarian.

'I think so, thanks,' said Cerian. She caught the bus home. Several times on the way she got out the piece of paper with the three addresses. She could just give it to Dylan. Only he was in a funny mood, she wasn't sure he wouldn't throw it away. And it would be good to surprise him, to say, I've found your mother, she's expecting you. But then maybe Dylan's mother wouldn't be all that pleased . . . And there was the problem of finding out which of the three was the right Catherine Elizabeth. She'd have to think up some excuse to call . . .

Dylan took a bus into the centre of town, looking for somewhere to get dry. It rained differently in Wales, sideways and upwards as well as down. Maybe he could invent a Welsh umbrella that you zipped up all round with just your feet sticking out.

He went over a bridge and came out in a covered shopping precinct by a bowling alley. He hung around there for a while, watching, thought of playing but decided it wouldn't be much fun on his own. He passed a multi-screen cinema but either he'd seen the films or they were for over 18s and he wouldn't be allowed in. At the other end of the precinct was a huge greenhouse. He attached himself to a family group and went in with them. No point in paying if he could get in for free. At least it was warm in there, very warm, he should soon dry off.

It was like a jungle, with massive palm trees and creepers and tropical birds calling and a gorilla made out of bits of metal lurking in the greenery. At the back was a bit with Venus fly-traps, but none of them were eating flies. And then there was another part with cacti. It was hot and dry in that bit but Dylan didn't stay long because he had cacti at what used to be home and these reminded him. As he came through the glass door back into the jungle, sprinklers came on and soaked him all over again. Feeling he'd grow webbed feet if he stayed in Wales, he went back into the cactus room to dry off. Then, the other side of the moat which ran round the outside of the greenhouse, he saw a police car draw up. Two policemen got out and started to walk towards the entrance.

He had to get out before he was trapped. He ran into the jungle, ducking and weaving among the plants and the people, bumped into someone, nearly fell, lurched on as somebody yelled after him. He slid through the door, saw the policemen in the entrance hall, whisked into the exhibition room and hid behind a screen. From below the screen he watched the navy-clad legs, standing, not moving, then slowly heading in his direction. He chose his moment, shot out behind the policemen, through the exit and away, running, zigzagging through the cars, not daring to look behind, sure he could hear pursuing feet behind the drumming of his heart and his breath gasping. A road, three lanes of traffic each way, no time for the crossing, running full tilt, horns blaring all round, a rush of hot air from a lorry that just missed him. Then he was over, down a side street, collapsed in a heap behind a wall. Then a siren, a blue light flashing, and he was up and running again; lurched round a corner, almost crashed into someone, tripped and fell headlong. He gazed in white-faced horror up from black lace-ups past black stockings to navy skirt, navy jacket to white hat. 'You all right, love?' asked the policewoman. 'You want to look where you're going.'

'S-sorry,' Dylan stammered, picked himself up and walked on.

He found himself in the marina, with sailing boats moored all round, ropes twanging against the masts like bells across the water.

The policewoman had sounded kind, had called him love. She didn't know he was a criminal. Maybe the two policemen hadn't been after him either . . . But then Cerian had said his picture was in the paper. He walked on, as the rain plastered his hair to his head and trickled down his neck, selecting from all the boats the one he would own to sail away forever.

Dylan ducked under the barbed wire, through into the next field and up on to the ridge. It had finally stopped raining and the sky was clear. Below him the lights of Swansea gleamed; beyond, in the middle of the bay, was a full moon, lipping the water, spreading a dull silver track across the waves. To the right, the lighthouse pierced the blackness, four pulses, then dark.

He turned and went down towards the farmhouse and whatever the night might bring.

There was rain lashing against the window. Beth, chin on hands, watched as the drops hit, spread and trickled down the glass. Beyond, leafless branches flailed in the wind.

Beth sighed, stood up, walked across to the cot. The baby slept in red-faced concentration.

Then, out of the rain, Dylan heard voices. A sudden gust of wind guttered the candles as the door opened and slammed to. Geraint came in and behind him another man.

'Beth, this is Evan Thomas. I'm taking him on to help with the stock.'

Beth and the newcomer murmured a formal greeting, then turned away. But then, at the same instant, they both turned back. Their eyes met, and they smiled.

CHAPTER ELEVEN

Saturday 27 July

Next day Dylan woke to sunshine. It had been a dry night, raining only in his dreams. He lay for a while, trying to make sense of the things in his head. Then he gave up and went to look for Cerian.

When he arrived, Tom was unloading the van. ''Fraid she's out,' he grunted, heaving at a plastic sack of clay. 'But if you'll give me a hand I'll make you a cup of tea. Here, you take these.'

Dylan found himself carrying armfuls of paper bags labelled things like *Magnesium dioxide* and *Iron filings*. He and Tom toiled to and fro between the van and the studio, getting hot and dirty.

'Phew!' Tom dumped the last load of clay and wiped his hand across his forehead. 'I'm stocking up. If I can get this Japanese order my fortune's made.' He went to put the kettle on. 'I don't know where Cerian's gone. No one ever tells me anything. You can have Barkis, though. He'd be glad of a walk.'

Dylan drank his tea, then, for the want of anything better to do, set off with the dog. To his surprise, Barkis led him off at high speed, heading not towards the fields, nor towards the city centre, but along a street Dylan hadn't been down before.

They turned a corner and the reason for the dog's enthusiasm was revealed. A butcher's shop. Barkis practically broke into a run for the last few yards. He stopped dead in the doorway and sat down, blocking the exit. Dylan heaved at him, but he was not to be moved.

Over the dog's unbudgeable bulk he saw the butcher, a

big man in a blood-stained apron, advancing on him. 'I'm s-sorry,' he said, 'I can't shift him.'

'That's all right, lad. Barkis and me are mates, aren't we, boy?' He clouted the St Bernard's ample bottom, then held out an enormous bone.

Barkis closed his enormous teeth around it—quite gently—and then was off. Dylan, towed behind, twisted round to call thank you. The butcher was standing, hands on hips, laughing.

Two right turns and a quick left and they arrived at the park. Barkis ground to a halt, subsided on to the grass, and started chewing, crunching the bone in a series of ear-splitting cracks.

A family came by, with a baby in a buggy and a toddler who wobbled across the grass straight towards Barkis then, when the dog looked at him, started wailing. 'Can't you control that animal?' snapped the mother, scooping up her sobbing child.

'He didn't do anything,' said Dylan, indignant.

'It's a disgrace,' said the woman. 'Disgusting. Shouldn't be allowed, savage animal like that . . . ' Her complaints died into the distance.

Barkis carried on chewing. After a while, temporarily replete, he put the bone down and laid his head in Dylan's lap, drooling lovingly.

'You're slobbering all over me,' said Dylan, pushing him away. 'You should have a bib.'

Barkis gave him a mournful look, then got up and padded over to a rose-bed, carrying the bone. He began to dig a hole.

'Barkis!' called Dylan. 'Here! Stop it.'

The dog just carried on digging.

'Stop it!' Dylan went over and yanked at the dog's collar.

Barkis, getting really interested in his hole now, dug faster. A rose-bush tilted to one side.

Dylan, panicking, looked round. Fortunately there was no one about. He stuffed the lead into his pocket and went to sit on a bench some way off, trying to look as if the dog was nothing to do with him.

Out of the corner of his eye he saw a rose-bush fly through the air.

'Hey! You!'

Dylan turned to see a boy of around his own age, but bigger, confronting him.

'You're the boy who nicked Andy's bike!'

'I didn't;' said Dylan.

'You did! I saw you!'

'I only borrowed it. I was bringing it back.'

'You're lying. You're a thief, and a liar, and I'm going to sort you out.'

The boy made a grab for Dylan's shirt, hauled him to his feet, then suddenly dropped him as Barkis, growling, hackles up, charged. Turning to run, the boy found himself pinned against a tree, the dog's fearsome teeth inches from his face. 'Call him off!' he screamed.

'Okay, Barkis,' said Dylan, hooking his fingers into the dog's collar. 'Let him go.'

The boy twisted aside and fled.

'Well done, Barkis,' said Dylan, letting out a long sigh of relief. 'Thank you.'

Barkis, wearing a satisfied air, went back to his inter-rupted hole.

Cerian had got up early that morning. The first Catherine Elizabeth Hughes was right the other side of Swansea, two buses away. Fortunately it was Saturday, pocket-money day.

On the bus Cerian rehearsed her story.

She didn't quite have the courage to turn up on a stranger's doorstep and ask her if she was Dylan's mother. But she needed to talk to her for long enough to find out if it was a possibility. She decided to pretend she was from abroad, maybe from the States, she could do a good American accent, and to be looking for a long-lost aunt.

By the time she reached the bus station she had run the

scenario through three times, adding more cunning questions each time and each time eliciting more information. She would, she decided, as she sat on a bench waiting for the bus to Bon-y-maen, make a fantastic enquiry agent. She would have an office in London, just off Mayfair, with a brass plate that said *Cerian Rhys, Investigator: No Task Too Difficult.*

On the bus, it occurred to her that although she could ask the right questions, Mrs Hughes might not give the right answers. She re-ran the scene and this time finished up being told to go away before the police were called.

Walking down the main street of Bon-y-maen she thought suddenly that Mrs Hughes might be out. For a moment she felt relieved, then conscience-stricken. Dylan needed her help and she mustn't be a coward.

It was hot but windy. A chip paper, scudding along the pavement, wrapped itself round her ankle. Clouds were weaving along the top of the tree-clad hills to her left, above the houses.

She asked her way from a woman with a push-chair. The woman pushed her hair out of her eyes and stopped to think. Bottom of the hill, the turning by the newsagents, then first left—or did she mean right? She held up each hand in turn. That way, anyway. Cerian thanked her and walked on.

Too soon she found herself on an estate of brick-and-pebbledash houses. Number 19 was tucked away in a corner, behind lace curtains. No clues.

She walked past the house twice, then muttering, 'Cerian Rhys, Investigator' to herself, summoned up all her determination and turned up the garden path.

There was no answer to her knocking, not for a minute or two, then suddenly the clink of a chain being removed. The door swung open to reveal an old lady, all pink: pink dress, pink face, pink scalp over which sparse white hair was stretched with pink curlers. Her hand shot out, clasped Cerian's arm, drew her in. 'Come in, come in, I'm glad you came so soon, I've been that worried.'

71

Cerian, once in the hall, towered over her. 'They've been hanging there for days,' said the old lady. 'I went to the council but they wouldn't do anything. There and you've caught me with my curlers in, such a state I am.'

Confused but undaunted, Cerian embarked on her explanation, in her best American accent, of how she'd come from Los Angeles . . .

The old lady gazed at her for a moment, then broke in. 'It's so difficult since my husband died. I daren't go out at night, not with them hanging there, and I hear them screeching sometimes, just like on the television, I saw the programme last week, did you see it?'

Obviously she hadn't heard a word Cerian had said. 'Come on through, the ladder's in the garage.' She caught Cerian's arm again and towed her through the kitchen and out of the back door. Any hope Cerian had that Catherine Elizabeth had moved away went when she saw, lying on the kitchen table, a pension book labelled Mrs C. E. Hughes.

'When my husband was alive we had a car, but then all good things come to an end, don't they, and I've still got the ladders. Look, up there, can you see them?' She pointed to the apex of the roof, some thirty feet up, where Cerian could vaguely make out a dark shape.

'What is it?'

'*Bats*, I'm telling you, just like on the television. Here, we'll get the ladder and you can get rid of them, nasty things, I'm that afraid, what if they came in the house?'

'It doesn't look like bats,' said Cerian doubtfully, 'and anyway it's good to have bats, they eat lots of insects and they don't do any harm. I wish we had them in our house.' But Mrs Hughes, busy opening the garage door, didn't hear her. There were three ladders in the garage. The old lady seized one end of the longest, which was wooden and, as Cerian realized when she picked up the other end, horribly heavy.

'I'm sure it's illegal to hurt bats,' said Cerian. 'They're protected.'

'I can't be bothered with that,' said Mrs Hughes. 'At my age *I* need protecting. Come on, one, two, three . . . '

Puffing and grunting they carried the ladder out into the drive and dropped it. 'It opens up,' said Mrs Hughes, tugging at one end, to no avail.

'Maybe it opens the other way,' shouted Cerian.

'No, this way,' said Mrs Hughes, determined but still ineffective. At last she gave up, baffled. Cerian pulled in the opposite direction and, bumpily, in fits and starts, the ladder extended.

'There we are,' said Mrs Hughes, triumphant.

But getting twenty feet of heavy wooden ladder up against the wall was like wrestling with a whale. To and fro they tottered, the ladder swinging crazily, with a life of its own. It missed the kitchen window by inches, pushed Cerian back into the garage, almost squashed Mrs Hughes against the gate, then crashed against the wall. Cerian leaned against it, panting. Wordlessly, beyond words, she gestured to Mrs Hughes to come the other side, then, pushing the ladder against the wall, gradually levered it upright. From there she pulled the bottom out bit by bit until eventually the ladder stood propped at a reasonable angle in roughly the right place. Eyes closed, chest heaving, she waited for the world to stop quaking.

'Here you are.' Mrs Hughes had darted back into the garage and come back with a broom. She thrust it at Cerian. 'Up you go. I'll hold the bottom.'

Clutching the broom, still panting, Cerian started up the ladder. It bounced as she climbed. One of the rungs rotated, nearly sliding her off. It was a very old ladder. Stopping for a rest about twelve feet up she saw the pin-prick holes of woodworm. She looked down. Mrs Hughes, her foot on the bottom rung, was grasping the sides of the ladder as if her frail weight could make any difference. If I fall off, thought Cerian, if the ladder breaks, I'll probably flatten her.

'Can you see them?' called Mrs Hughes.

Cerian looked up. Now she was closer she could make

out what it was she was supposed to be removing. 'It's not
bats,' she shouted. 'It's half a house-martins' nest.'

'What's that?'

'A house-martins' nest.'

'What are they?'

'Birds. Small birds.'

'Ugh. Horrible. Go on, get rid of them.'

'But they're nice.'

'No, they're not. What if they came in the house?'

'They won't.'

'No, no, get rid of them.'

'They can't hurt you,' said Cerian, 'and they have to live
somewhere, poor things.'

'What do you mean, poor things? It's me who's the poor
thing. Terrified of them I am.'

'And you're not supposed to destroy nests. I know that,
our neighbours . . . '

But Mrs Hughes wasn't listening. 'Get rid of them,' she
said, ruthless. 'I'm not having nasty creatures on my wall.'

Cerian gave up arguing and carried on climbing. The
ladder bucked and bowed beneath her feet. I wonder, she
thought, clinging desperately, if Mrs Hughes is as scared as
I am.

When she dared climb no further she latched her left arm
round the ladder and poked the broom upwards. She wasn't
high enough. One more rung, eyes fixed on the pebbledash.

She looked up again. At least it was only half a nest, and
it didn't look fresh. The martins must have decided to move
elsewhere. She didn't blame them.

She swung the broom in a wild arc. It hit the nest, which
exploded in a shower of dried mud.

Mrs Hughes was beaming, despite the mud in her hair,
when Cerian slithered back down to the ground.

'Thank you, dear. Now I'll be able to sleep in my bed at
night.'

Getting the ladder down was marginally easier than
getting it up, which was just as well as Cerian was worn out.
Mrs Hughes, though, seemed as spry as ever. 'Thank you,

dear. I'm very grateful. When you get to my age you can't be having horrid screechy things flapping round.'

'How old are you?' The question lacked subtlety, Cerian thought, but she was past caring.

'Bless you, dear, I'm eighty-eight next birthday.' Mrs Hughes heaved the ladder back into its place in the garage and dusted her hands with satisfaction. 'Now then, would you like a cup of tea?'

It was hours before Cerian escaped, after three cups of tea and a plate of iced fancies. And for all that Mrs Hughes had talked almost non-stop, Cerian still didn't know which of her many relations the old lady thought she was.

Walking back to the bus-stop she wondered what Mrs Hughes would make of it when the real relation turned up.

Oh well, she thought, at least I know she's too old to be Dylan's mother. One down, two to go.

Cerian was still out when Dylan returned Barkis, grubby about the paws and drooling more spectacularly than ever. I suppose she's gone off to see her mates, he thought. Forgotten all about me. Well, see if I care. He kicked some nettles. A butterfly flew up, twirled round, disappeared into the sun.

The Chinese takeaway was just opening and smelled good. Dylan bought sweet-and-sour pork and fried rice and sat on a wall to eat it with his fingers and his Swiss army knife. Then he wiped his knife and his fingers on his jeans and looked at his watch. Half past seven.

Slowly, by a roundabout route, he headed back to the farmhouse.

Beth, the child balanced on her hip, was walking into the pigsty. Dylan followed her. Chickens scurried out from under their feet. She stopped by one of the stalls, where a vast sow lay on its side, a row of piglets grunting and kicking at its teats.

A figure loomed out of the shadows at the end of the building. 'Were you looking for me?'

'Oh—oh, Evan, you gave me a fright. I wasn't expecting anyone . . . I just came in to look at the pigs.'

'You like pigs?'

'Yes. I reared one, he used to follow me everywhere. I still miss him. I expect you think me foolish.'

'No. They're intelligent animals. You can get attached.'

She nodded, moved down to the next stall, then the next.

'Mind—it's dirty down the end,' said Evan.

'It doesn't look dirty.' He was barring her way. 'Are you trying to hide something?'

He shrugged and moved aside. In the last stall were two young sows. And something dark in the straw. Beth leaned forward to see what it was.

Curled up was a tabby cat under a pile of kittens.

'Are you hiding them from Geraint?'

'It seems a shame to drown them.'

'Don't worry, I shan't tell.'

They stood side by side, looking at the heap of multi-coloured fur, from which rose a steady purring.

The baby reached out and caught hold of Evan's jacket. 'Oh—I'm sorry.' Beth tried to free the material from the baby's grasping fingers.

Evan was looking down at her.

She looked up at him, flushed, pulled the baby away and hurried out.

Evan stood looking after her.

CHAPTER TWELVE
Sunday 28 July

Dylan sat on the stile and gazed down at the sea. It was a perfect morning, blue and still. The bay lay like silk.

Every time he passed, he stopped here to look at the view. Every time it was different. It was, he thought, a bit like when he'd been on holiday in Switzerland, only there it was a mountain that dominated the town. You were always looking at the mountain, and it was always changing. In Swansea it was the bay, the sea coming in and out, clouds, wind and light.

He walked on down to Cerian's house.

But when he rang the doorbell he was answered with a lot of silence. No footsteps. No dog barking. No van.

He walked slowly back down the path. What was he going to do now? The worst thing about running away was how boring it was.

As the gate creaked open he heard a sudden 'prrrp' and something furry wound round his legs. Mulligan. Dylan stooped to pick her up. The cat burrowed into his arms, purring ecstatically, rubbed her cheek against his nose and licked his neck. Her tongue was hot, rough, and it hurt.

Abruptly she had had enough. Back paws thumping against Dylan's chest, she leapt down and began to walk along the road, tail up. Then she stopped, turned her head, and miaowed.

Dylan followed her. She walked on. He picked her up again, took her back to the house, put her down on the wall. 'Stay there. You'll get lost.'

She jumped down and set off along the road again.

Several times Dylan caught her, took her back. Each time she refused to stay.

In the end he gave up and let her take him for a walk. It

wasn't like going for a walk with a dog, though. For a while she would step sedately, only the tip of her upright tail twitching. Then suddenly she would vanish, reappearing only after he had panicked that she never would, and from a quite unexpected direction.

She explored the inside of a skip, from which she emerged with black smudges on her ginger fur. Then there was a tumultuous chirping as two sparrows squabbled in the dust, and she pounced. The birds flew up and Mulligan seemed to fly with them, arcing through the air, then they were all in a tree screaming abuse at each other. The sparrows flew away, leaving Mulligan complaining that this branch was high, high, and how could she possibly be expected to get down?

'Jump!' called Dylan. 'Come on!'

But she only sat and miaowed.

Eventually, Dylan decided he'd have to climb up and get her. He hauled himself up on to the nearby wall, eyed the distance to the lowest branch, crouched, and jumped. He caught the branch with one hand, swung, got the other hand on, wriggled his feet up the trunk, heaved, scrabbled and somehow managed to get himself into a sitting position. Panting, he discovered that Mulligan had jumped down and was walking quietly up the road.

Her next disappearance was even longer than usual. And when she returned, leaping over a garden wall, she was carrying a kipper. A whole one.

'Oh no,' wailed Dylan, making a grab at her but missing. She trotted smartly down the road, head held high and a little to one side, so as not to drag the fish in the dust.

Dylan peered over the garden wall for signs of pursuit. No one was coming. Sighing with relief, he followed after the cat burglar. Coming to a piece of waste ground, she settled under a bush and started to eat. Dylan sat on a rock, waiting.

There was a stirring in the undergrowth. He watched, expecting a blackbird, or maybe a mouse. Mulligan was watching too, one eye cocked while she carried on chewing.

The grass parted and a small black face appeared. Green eyes, and a pink tongue as the mouth opened in a soundless miaow.

Mulligan stopped eating for long enough to hiss.

The kitten crouched down in the dust, eyes fixed on the kipper. It was black all over, except for four very dirty white paws and an equally grubby white chin. The end of its tail twitched.

The fish was disappearing fast. Like toothpaste squeezed from a tube, the kitten oozed closer. And pounced.

There was a tumbling in the dust. When it settled, the kitten was gone and Mulligan and the kipper were further under the bush.

'Mulligan!' said Dylan reproachfully. 'Poor little thing, he's starving. Come on, you can share.' Slowly he started to crawl forwards.

The kitten watched, peering out from behind a rusty oil drum.

Dylan carried on crawling till he was under the bush. He stretched out a hand. Mulligan spat.

'Come on,' said Dylan. 'Just a bit.' He edged closer.

Mulligan discovered an itch on her back and twisted round to lick it.

Closer still.

Mulligan yawned. Disclaiming all interest in the kipper, she settled down for a thorough wash.

Dylan picked up the remains of the fish before she could change her mind and wriggled out from under the bush. The kitten was still peering out from behind the oil drum. Dylan called to him, holding out a piece of kipper.

With a sudden swoop, the kitten was there and the titbit had vanished. Dylan offered more, piece by piece. The kitten ate ravenously, then nosed Dylan's fingers away and set to to lick the bones clean. Soon all that was left was a cartoon sketch of a fish's skeleton, each bone bare and gleaming. Cautiously Dylan reached out. The kitten trapped his hand and licked the fingers thoroughly, pink tongue rasping.

When all the fish, the last lick of taste of fish, was gone, the kitten walked into Dylan's arms, curled up and went to sleep.

Mulligan too was sleepy: it had been a demanding morning and now—she yawned. Dylan scooped her up as well and carried the two young cats back to Cerian's house.

There was still no one in. Mulligan retired to a patch of shade to resume her interrupted sleep. Dylan stood on the pavement wondering what to do.

'Well,' he said slowly, 'I suppose you're mine now.' The kitten slept on. His nose and whiskers twitched. Dreaming of kippers, perhaps.

Dylan went to buy some cat food.

Cerian rode along the Mumbles bike path. It was crowded with trippers and she had constantly to ring her bell and weave in and out of walkers too stupid to move over.

The fatter the bottom, the skimpier the shorts, she thought. Just because they were on holiday, people thought it was all right to go round wobbling wodges of naked flesh.

She rang her bell again, and again. Four women strung out across the path, totally ignoring her. She rang again, shouted 'Excuse me.' They finally turned round but by that time she'd had to stop. One of the women, fat in pink shorts and straw hat, looked her up and down. 'Are bicycles *allowed* on here?' she enquired in an English drawl.

'Yes,' said Cerian. 'They usually are on bike paths.'

Fuming, she rode on. I hate tourists, she thought. Summer Sundays were always the worst. Grockles in droves, cluttering up the place, always complaining. 'The beach is *muddy*,' they'd grumble. 'Dirty. Not safe.' As if they expected it freshly laundered before their visit. As if it wasn't home to gulls and oystercatchers and flitting waves of waders and dogs and joggers. No one had a right to criticize who hadn't seen it in January, sand scudding in the wind, waves like black lace, sunset silver across the gleaming shoals; who hadn't walked off a million bad moods in all the changing moods of the sea.

It was hot. The tide was far out, the sand shimmering in haze. She negotiated the slalom by the boating pool, then the path straightened, ran between intermittent trees, patches of alternate heat and shade. The warm breeze smelt of salt seaweed and privet hedge.

When she reached Mumbles she stopped for an ice cream. She felt she needed cooling down before she tackled Catherine Elizabeth Hughes II. She sat on the sea wall to eat it: raspberry flavour and delicious. Cerian Rhys, Investigator, licked her fingers and set off on the next stage of her enquiry.

The main street was packed, but as soon as she turned up a side road the crowds vanished. Geraniums in hanging baskets, cats in sunny windows.

The house she was looking for was white, with green shutters, set back from the road behind a garden full of lupins and delphiniums and honeysuckle. It looked promising. Whoever lived here had to be nice.

She leaned her bike against the porch and knocked: a brass knocker shaped like a dolphin.

A man opened the door. She stared, speechless suddenly.

'Yes?' he asked encouragingly.

'Um—does Mrs Hughes live here? Mrs Catherine Elizabeth Hughes?' She remembered her American accent.

He smiled. 'Yes, she does. She's not down yet, though, doesn't believe in getting up too early on a Sunday. Can I help?'

'I—um—I really need to speak to her. Will she be long? Can I wait?'

'Yes, I expect she'll be down soon. You'd better come in.'

He showed her into a sitting-room with chairs covered in flowery fabric and pot plants everywhere. 'Please—sit down.'

Cerian perched on the edge of the sofa, desperately trying to think what to say. He was about the right age, small, wiry, curly hair and gilt-framed glasses. He looked friendly but a husband was a complication she hadn't considered.

He sat watching her. 'So—why do you want to see my wife?'

A deep breath. Cerian took the plunge. 'Well, you see, I've just come over to Britain, from the States, that is. And I thought, well, gee, I thought I'd just have to look up my folks while I'm here. I just love it here, your Wales is so cute, all those historic castles and those dinky little mountains and . . .'

'And you think my wife is a relation of yours?' He looked—amused—almost as if he was laughing at her. Though she was sure there was nothing wrong with her accent.

'Well, I sure hope so. You see, my Mom, she came from little old Wales and she always used to talk about the folks back home, specially her sister. Catherine Elizabeth, she was, and she married a man called Hughes, Mom said.' Cerian felt she was really getting into the part now, if only the man would stop grinning.

'Right,' he said. 'I'll give her a call.' He went out.

Cerian gazed round the room, trying to deduce things from the bric-à-brac. No photos; some hand-made porcelain, not bad but not as good as her Dad's; books on accounting, prehistory, music, alternative medicine, yoga.

Mr Hughes came back in. 'She'll be down in a minute.' He sat in a rocking-chair and continued to watch her thoughtfully while rocking to and fro.

The clock on the mantelpiece was painted with a picture of a gate, and each time the clock ticked a sheep jumped over. Once she started looking at it she couldn't take her eyes away. The clock ticked, the rocking-chair creaked, the sheep jumped . . .

The door opened. The woman who came in was tall, slim and very beautiful. And black. 'Well, hi,' she said. 'So you think I might be your auntie.'

And she laughed. And her husband laughed. They laughed so much they had to prop each other up.

Mrs Hughes was the first to recover. 'I'm sorry, child, but if you could see your face . . .' She wiped her streaming eyes.

82

Cerian headed towards the door, saying stiffly, 'I'm sorry I troubled you.'

'No trouble.' Mrs Hughes laid a hand on Cerian's shoulder and smiled. 'You made my day. Stay and have a cup of tea if you like.'

'And tell us all about it,' said her husband cordially. 'Who you're looking for and where you got that cute little American accent.'

'No, thank you. It's a private investigation. I shall have to be going now.' On her dignity.

They accompanied her to the front door. Still on her dignity she pushed her bike down the path, mounted and rode away.

Half-way back to Swansea she started to grin. Then to laugh. Jangling her bell, giggling like a maniac, she weaved her way through the flocks of sun-pink grockles.

The kitten slept a lot. Dylan discovered that if he half-zipped his cotton jacket it made a sort of kangaroo pouch where the kitten curled up, eyes closed, motionless except when nose and paws twitched in a dream.

It was a fine evening, too warm and light to think of sleeping yet. Dylan decided to go and have another look at the badger sett, wait and watch for the badgers to come out.

Inside the wood it was still, cosy as a bed. The grasses brushed soft against his legs. Sunlight dappled the leaves, fresh and clean after yesterday's rain.

There were tracks in the loose earth outside the sett entrances. Five claws: badger.

Dylan moved away, settled down with his back against a tree close to the broadest track, fidgeted for a while until he found a comfortable position, then went still. In the silence the smallest noises grew. A cricket, zithering. A bumble bee, droning. A stem collapsed under the bee's weight as it landed. Rustling as a beetle stirred the dry leaves. Tentative, a pigeon cooed.

He became aware of eyes staring at him. Slowly he turned his head. Uphill about twenty yards, sitting watching him, was a fox. Red against the brown earth, and, behind it, the darkness of a hole. Dylan sat motionless, hardly breathing. Gradually the alertness went out of the fox's position. Soon it was just sitting, quiet in the evening light.

Then footsteps. Dylan turned his head the other way, twisting as far as he could go. Round the rough bark of the tree he saw a second fox trotting down the track. It had something in its mouth. Suddenly it saw him and in one fluid movement had turned and fled.

The first fox had vanished as well. No sign of the badgers. Too early yet, the light still strong. Dylan leaned back into the tree and dozed.

Slowly, the light began to fade.

And then, again, he heard footsteps behind him. Again he turned, and saw, not a badger, nor a fox, but a woman wrapped in a cloak. Beth. She hurried down the track, her breath coming fast, just a few feet away from him so that he felt the stir of her passing. Out of the darkness by the sett rose another figure, his face flushed by a last ray from the setting sun. Evan. He held out his hand, drew Beth to him, down into the shadows.

There was movement in the dark, whispers below hearing, pale gleams in the blackness. The hair stood up on the back of Dylan's neck.

Then in moonlight he could see again, and the figures took shape. Black and white and a flurry of grey, rolling to and fro, two badgers playing in front of the sett.

CHAPTER THIRTEEN
Monday 29 July

Dylan woke scratching. He had little red marks all over his chest. At first he thought he had measles, then he noticed that the kitten was scratching too. He grabbed hold of him in mid-scratch and investigated his fur. There were lots of shiny brown things scurrying about. Fleas. The kitten had fleas. In fact, they both did.

'Right,' said Dylan, 'I'm taking you to a vet.'

The kitten purred, as if to say he was happy to go anywhere only—he wound in and out of Dylan's legs—it was hours and *hours* since he'd eaten and please could he have breakfast first?

Dylan opened another can of cat food.

They went for a swim first. Dylan stripped to his underpants, then left the kitten guarding his clothes as he walked into the sea. The kitten squeaked a protest, panicked at all this wet stuff that kept chasing him up the beach, then sidetracked by the smell of a dead crab, then entranced by a piece of dry seaweed that danced and flew and landed and danced again.

Dylan swam straight out as fast as he could go, then, in case the fleas had moved up to his head, dived and sat on the bottom.

Then, swimming on his back, he looked at the sky and thought of Beth. He was still not sure what he had seen the previous evening: badgers, yes, and foxes, but as for the rest . . .

And whatever he had seen he didn't know what he thought about it.

But the badgers had been great. It was the best view he'd

ever had of them—he'd never before caught more than a glimpse of something running away in the darkness.

When he walked up out of the sea, the kitten was stalking a herring gull which turned and glared from a malevolent yellow eye. Dylan clapped his hands and the gull took off into an unhurried glide, wing-tips almost brushing the tops of the waves.

Dylan shook his clothes thoroughly and dressed. He felt cleaner, less itchy, though gritty from the sand. He picked up the kitten, who had his head in an old tin can, and headed up the beach. The flowers were covered in butterflies which flew off when he approached. Dylan thought, the only reason we can get close to plants is that they don't have legs to run away with. If they did . . . Maybe some people would have a pet birch or a tame hawthorn, but vegetables would be difficult to catch. Sunday mornings, the streets would be full of people chasing their grass with lawn-mowers. And some plants would be faster than others—runner beans, for instance; while potatoes would have to wade through a tangle of tubers. And there would be dangerous plants. Like rhinos, approach at your peril. Imagine being chased by a giant redwood . . . or Venus fly-traps might grow big enough to eat people, and lie in wait with sticky tendrils . . .

There was a post office on a corner. Dylan took his place in the queue, behind two girls who were talking about hairdressers. One had very long hair with beads plaited in. He wondered how far fleas could jump. The kitten woke up, yawned, stood on Dylan's arm, stretched.

The girl shook her head. The beads dangled alluringly. The kitten prodded them.

'Ow!' The girl turned angrily. 'Oh, how *sweet*!'

'He's got fleas,' said Dylan.

'Ugh!' She backed off.

'What have you got there?' asked the man behind the counter when Dylan's turn came.

'He's a stray. I'm looking after him. Can you tell me where there's a vet, please?'

The man lifted the hatch, reached through and tickled the kitten's ears while he gave directions. 'It'll cost you, mind.'

'That's all right,' said Dylan.

The vet's had just opened for morning surgery when Dylan arrived. The waiting-room was full, mostly of dogs, and a few cats in baskets, glaring balefully. The kitten, after a brief struggle, buried himself in Dylan's armpit. Dylan squeezed in between a spaniel of sorts and a border collie.

An armed truce prevailed, on the whole. There was an occasional bark, checked by an owner's sharp command. Otherwise it was quiet, just the panting of dogs who wanted to be elsewhere. Every few minutes the surgery door would open and a relieved animal would come out, claws clattering on the tiled floor, while a reluctant one was taken in. A golden labrador had to be dragged, sitting on its broad behind, across the polished floor.

Most of the pets had not just an owner, but a whole anxious family with them. A small fair-haired girl went in to the surgery clutching a tortoise and accompanied by mother, father, brother and sister. It must be pretty difficult to treat a tortoise, Dylan thought, especially if the tortoise didn't want to be treated.

At last it was his turn. He went in, groped under his armpit and extracted the kitten.

The vet was a woman, quite young.

'He's got fleas,' said Dylan.

'Hmm.' She held the kitten down on the table, felt him all over, peered into his eyes, ears, mouth, picked him up and checked under his tail, took his temperature. He opened his mouth to miaow but no sound came out. 'How long have you had him?'

'I just got him. He's a stray.'

'Hmm,' she said again. She got out a stethoscope, listened to the kitten's chest, then let go. Instantly he climbed back into Dylan's arms. 'He's got fleas, worms, canker in his ears, I don't like the sound of his chest, he's malnourished and should really still be with his mother. Chances are he won't survive.'

'Yes, he will. I'll make him.'

The vet looked at him thoughtfully. 'I've three litters of healthy kittens out the back,' she said. 'They all need homes. You could take your pick.'

Dylan's mouth set in a straight line. 'Could you give him some medicine, please,' he said.

'Okay. Let's have him back on the table.' She fetched bottles from the shelf. 'I'll show you how to use these, but what he needs most of all is lots of TLC.'

'What's that?'

'Tender Loving Care. You'll have to look after him as if you were his mother.'

'Right,' said Dylan.

There was a spray for the fleas, a tablet for the worms, drops for the canker, and an injection just in case. The kitten bore it all patiently, until the vet put the drops in his ears. Then he opened his mouth in an outraged squeak. Dylan giggled. 'Why can't he miaow?'

'Sometimes they don't.' She let the patient go and smiled as he snuggled back inside Dylan's jacket, leaving the end of his wispy tail hanging out.

'How much will that be, please?'

'Oh—umm . . . ' She hesitated.

'I've got money.'

'Well then, shall we say £3?'

He handed over the coins and tucked the medicines into his pocket.

'What are you going to call him?' asked the vet.

Dylan, who had been giving a lot of thought to the question, suddenly knew. 'Lucky,' he said.

'Right. Good luck, Lucky.'

On the way back, Dylan stopped at a pet shop and bought a catnip mouse. Under his armpit, Lucky purred.

Cerian woke dreaming, tried to remember but, as ever, the dream slipped through the fingers of her mind.

The sun slithered through the curtains, promising summer for ever. Bed was warm and soft.

She lay listening to the Monday morning noises. Washing machine slooshing in the kitchen, clunks from the pottery, someone outside hammering. Barkis on the landing like a young steam train. She must have slept late.

Rolling over she gazed at the clock in disbelief. Half past ten. And today she had to see Catherine Elizabeth III.

Still, she was too comfortable to get up just yet . . .

At least she didn't have too far to go: she had kept the nearest to last. Last chance. Third time lucky? Maybe she should change her story, though. The niece from America hadn't worked too well.

She was still trying to think of a better story when she went down for breakfast and found the solution waiting for her. A letter, with a sponsorship form for the Walk for Wildlife. Perfect. Sponsorship forms were as good a pretext as Trick or Treat for tyrannizing the neighbourhood. C.E. III would have to put her name on the form, Cerian could have a good look at her and if she seemed a possible candidate could engage her in conversation. About . . . Oh well, she'd think of something. She swallowed a hasty bowl of bran flakes and fetched her bike.

Panting up Constitution Hill, she wished she'd left her bike at home. Cobbled, potholed, almost vertical. Presumably it got its name because walking up it was supposed to be good for the constitution. If you didn't drop dead in the process. She stopped to look at the view. Boats in the bay.

Terraces branched off on either side, running along the curve of the hill. There were houses only on one side, the up side of each terrace, the rows running in tiers like cinema seating, with the sea for a screen.

Glynderwen Terrace was near the top. She leaned on her bike and waited to get her breath back. On top of a high brick wall a tortoiseshell cat, paws tucked under, blinked at the sunshine. No. 23 was painted white. A flight of stone steps ran up to the front door between beds of roses and sprawling hydrangea.

There was an outer door standing open, an inner door with no bell. She knocked on the glass, waited, knocked again, harder.

'Looking for me?' asked a voice behind her. Carrying bags of Sainsbury's shopping up the steps was Dylan's mother.

'I'm looking for sponsors,' said Cerian, offering the form, going through the motions though now she had no need to. Dylan's mother looked just like him.

'Oh, goodness. Let me just put these bags down . . . ' She unlocked the door, dropped the bags in the hall, took the form. '2p a mile all right? I expect I'll have to sponsor half the neighbourhood.' She signed: C. E. Hughes.

Dylan returned from a visit to the badger sett (unproductive—the kitten's pouncings had made sure he saw neither badgers, nor foxes, nor anything else) to find a note on his sleeping-bag, weighed down by a stone.

'*Please come round tomorrow morning. I have something to tell you. Cerian.*' He read it twice, then shrugged, then remembered he hadn't given Lucky his ear drops this evening.

The kitten was getting to know what the little bottle meant and tried to escape, hiding in an old cardboard box where he went all flat. Dylan prised him out and held him down. Lucky squeaked indignantly and shook his head, spraying the drops in Dylan's face. Maybe I'll get Cerian to help tomorrow, thought Dylan, wiping his face on his sleeve.

He lay down to sleep but couldn't settle.

There was an owl hooting nearby. He wondered why owls hoot; you'd think it would scare all the mice and voles away. Bats flitted overhead. Do owls catch bats? Do cats catch bats? Lucky was so small it might be bats catching cats. Do *owls* catch cats? Stay here, safe, he said to the kitten, who was sleeping peacefully inside his jacket.

But for Dylan sleep was far away. He watched the

moonlight creep along the walls, listened to the night-time noises, and waited.

From the pigsty came the sound of laughter. Dylan went to investigate. Lucky stood up, eyes closed, turned round, then collapsed back in a heap.

Standing side by side, looking down into the far stall, were Evan and Beth. The kittens, bigger now, were climbing, chasing each other, pouncing on a stick that Evan was jiggling in the straw. The mother cat caught one of her offspring and started to wash it.

Lucky had woken now and sat motionless in Dylan's arms, staring saucer-eyed.

'Doesn't she look proud?' said Beth.

'So she should,' answered Evan. 'It's a fine family.' He had his arm around her waist, holding her tight.

They laughed as a kitten leapt for the tail of one of the sows and the startled pig cavorted across the stall, grunting.

They were making too much noise to hear Geraint coming. Dylan shouted an instinctive warning. His voice made no sound. Geraint brushed past him with a hot stale smell of sweat and horses.

Evan looked up. There was a silence.

Beth turned her head and looked into her husband's eyes.

91

CHAPTER FOURTEEN

Tuesday 30 July

Dylan was at Cerian's house early next morning. He had to dodge as Bea swept out of the gate, late for work as usual.

Cerian let him in. She was wearing an important look. 'What is it?' asked Dylan. 'Why the note?'

'Ssh!' she hissed melodramatically, then led him into the kitchen where Tom was eating breakfast.

'Morning,' said Tom. 'Porridge?'

'Please.' Dylan sat down. Lucky, lured by the smell of food, wriggled out of his jacket on to the table.

'Manners!' said Tom, scooping the kitten up in one enormous fist. 'No animals on the table while we're eating, *if* you please!' He held Lucky up, nose to nose, and grinned.

'Isn't he sweet!' cried Cerian, forgetting to be mysterious.

The kitten opened a pink mouth in silent protest. Tom dipped his finger in his porridge bowl and held it up to be licked.

There was a thud as Mulligan came in through the kitchen window. Tail like a bottle-brush, she expressed her opinion of interlopers. 'Manners,' said Tom again. 'That's no way to welcome guests.' Mulligan spat. Lucky, intent on Tom's porridge-laden finger, ignored her.

'They've met before,' said Dylan; and then he had to tell them how. Tom leaned back comfortably to listen, the kitten curled on his lap. Mulligan turned her back, registering disapproval in every hair. Cerian, watching the clock, fidgeted.

Tom seemed settled for the morning, launching into sagas of all the stray cats he had known.

Lucky was conducting a determined campaign to capture

Mulligan's tail, interspersed with attacks on various offending shoelaces.

'Are you doing any work this morning, Dad?' Cerian interrupted at last.

'Trying to get rid of me?'

'I just thought—it's half past eleven . . .'

'Already? Oh well, I suppose . . .' Eventually he wandered off into the studio. But he didn't stay there. Every time Cerian took a deep breath to tell Dylan the news, her father reappeared asking if she had seen this or done that.

At last Cerian had had enough. 'Come on, Dylan,' she said. 'Let's go for a walk.'

'Must we?' said Dylan. He seemed to spend most of his life walking at the moment; it was a change to sit in a chair.

'Yes,' said Cerian.

Dylan settled the kitten inside his shirt and followed her out.

'This way,' said Cerian. She set off uphill.

'Can't we go down the marina?' said Dylan.

'No. Come on.'

Dylan paused to rearrange Lucky, whose claws were stuck in his armpit, then ran after her. 'So what's the big mystery?'

Cerian stopped, looked all round, then whispered, 'I've found her.'

'Found who?'

'Your mother.' Dylan stared at her blankly. '*Catherine Elizabeth Hughes*,' she said. Still he just stared.

A great tide of panic swept through him. He felt sick.

'Well, say something,' said Cerian crossly. 'I thought you'd be grateful.'

'S-sorry,' muttered Dylan.

'She's very nice,' said Cerian, taking pity. 'She looks like you.'

'Looks like me?'

'That's what I said.'

'I've never met anyone who looks like me,' said Dylan slowly.

'Well, you're going to meet one now.'

'Now?'

'If she's in. It's not far.' Cerian took charge, leading Dylan who was still too numb with shock to ask how and who and why . . .

It took about half an hour to reach Catherine Elizabeth's house. Dylan, with London legs, panted up the hill.

'I'll—um—I'll hang around here,' said Cerian. 'I'll look after Lucky.'

'You're not coming in with me?'

'I don't think I'd better. Do you?'

'Suppose not.' Dylan swallowed and walked on up, towards the house.

On the corner he stopped, looking at the house which might have been so familiar. As he gazed the door opened. A boy ran down the steps, walked off, kicking a Coke can.

His brother? Dylan went cold. He was suddenly furiously jealous.

He marched the last few yards to the house, stormed up the steps and banged on the door.

A woman opened it. Dylan gaped. She really did look like him.

'I'm Dylan,' he said.

Her hand flew to her mouth. 'Oh God. Dear God.' She stood staring.

At last she said: 'You'd better come in.' She led him down a passage to a big kitchen. Dylan glimpsed a sitting-room, and another room piled high with boxes and bicycles, as he passed.

'Sit down,' she said. She stood staring at him, wordless. Then suddenly she turned and started ferreting in a drawer.

Dylan wanted to run away.

She found what she was looking for: an old brown envelope. She opened it, took out some photos, pushed them across the table to Dylan. They were pictures of a small baby. Dylan had seen some like them before.

'Your—mother—sent them. Your first Christmas.' She

took them back. 'Nothing since. Which was quite right really. I suppose.'

Silence.

'Do you like London?'

'It's all right.'

Silence again.

'Do you want a cup of tea?' she said. 'I don't even know if you drink tea.'

'Yeah. I like tea.'

She busied herself with the kettle.

'Do you take sugar?'

'No, I've given it up.'

'So have I.' She half grinned.

'Here.' She put a mug in front of Dylan. It had a picture of a hippo on it.

'Biscuit?'

He shook his head.

'Go on, they're Bourbon.'

'I'm not hungry,' he said. His stomach had contracted into a small tight ball.

There was a calendar on the wall, with space for appointments. It was crowded with things like 'G—dentist' and 'P—bowling' and 'school open day'. The room was cluttered with skateboards and swimming things and electronic games. There was a photograph on the dresser of his mother, with a man standing behind her and two children in front.

Dylan picked up one of the games and turned it on. Fleets of space craft moved across the screen. It beeped and whined and yammered when he shot a spaceship down.

'It's such a shock,' she said.

'Aren't you pleased to see me?' Dylan kept his eyes on the game.

'Of course—only I wasn't expecting . . . ' Her voice tailed away.

Dylan shot down another spaceship.

'Anyway,' she said brightly. 'Tell me about yourself.'

He shrugged. 'Nothing to say really.'

'No—no, I suppose . . . It's difficult, isn't it?'

Out of the corner of his eye he saw her push her hair back from her face, take a swallow of tea, turn and look at the clock.

'Dylan—oh God, I don't know what to do—look, I'm really sorry, but my daughter will be back any moment. Would you mind—I don't want to ask you to leave, only . . . Perhaps we could meet tomorrow?'

He looked at her. 'All right.'

'Where . . . ? Somewhere indoors, in case it rains . . . ' She thought for a moment. 'Do you know the Maritime Museum? Down in the marina?'

Dylan nodded.

'I'll see you there, upstairs. Eleven o'clock?'

He nodded again, stood up and went to the door, leaving his tea untouched.

On the step he paused. 'What should I call you?' he asked.

'Kate. Call me Kate. See you tomorrow.'

He turned, ran down the steps, down the road, away.

Cerian, hearing footsteps, looked up from the game of pounce she had been playing with Lucky. Dylan didn't look as happy as she'd thought: in fact he didn't look happy at all.

'How did it go?' she asked.

Dylan only shrugged, picked up Lucky and started off downhill.

'I thought she was nice,' persisted Cerian.

Still no reply.

'Are you hungry? Do you want to come round for some soup?'

He shook his head.

'Are you okay?'

'Leave me alone,' he said, and walked off.

Cerian glared after him. 'Huh!' she muttered. 'There's gratitude for you!'

Then, fair-minded, she excused him. After all, he had

just met his mother for the first time. He must be feeling pretty weird.

Dylan wandered for hours, trying to sort out the confusion in his head. But he still felt as muddled as ever when, after dark, he finally got back to Cwm Rhithiol. He fed Lucky but had nothing to eat himself. He still felt sick. He crawled into his sleeping-bag, curled up, closed his eyes and fell into a fretful sleep.

His eyes opened on a scream. He had seen this before.

Beth was crouched on a stool, the child by the hearth staring, Geraint turning, bearing down on her, fist raised.

'No, please, please, no,' she was whimpering, cringing away from him, her arms wrapped around her body.

Geraint stood glaring at her.

'I'm sorry.' She was sobbing now. 'I'm sorry. Oh, Geraint, please . . . ' She hugged her belly, head bowed.

At last he lowered his fist. 'I'm not having it. Do you hear? You'll not keep it. I'll not have that man's child in my house.'

The little boy started to cry.

Beth still crouched on the stool, rocking slowly from side to side.

CHAPTER FIFTEEN

Wednesday 31 July: Morning

Bea was having a tidying-up morning. Her usual view of housework was that it could wait until there was nothing better to do, so when she did get round to doing some, it really needed doing.

First, she emptied the cupboard under the stairs of boxes of cans, bottles and newspapers saved for recycling, and loaded them into the van ready to go down to the dump. She made several discoveries in the process—a pair of scissors, a handbag, some packets of seeds which had been given up for lost months before. She piled her trophies up in the hall, evicted several spiders, and Mulligan, from the cupboard and went to make a start on upstairs.

By this time, Bea had really got into the mood. She swept up the chaos in Cerian's room, stripped the bed, and in a fit of enthusiasm decided to turn the mattress.

As Bea heaved up the mattress she saw a newspaper lying underneath. Grunting, she pulled it out and dropped it on the floor behind her. She straightened the mattress, made up the bed with clean sheets, then, her arms clasping the pile of dirty washing, stooped to pick up the newspaper. 'HAVE YOU SEEN THIS BOY?' she read, above a photo of Dylan. She closed her eyes, appalled. How could she possibly have missed that?

Tom came out of the studio into the kitchen and almost collided with his wife.

'Where's Cerian?' she demanded.

'Gone swimming, I think,' said Tom.

'Have you seen Dylan today?'

Tom shook his head. 'No, why?'

'If you see him,' said Bea, '*keep him here*. Think of some

excuse, sit on his head if you have to, but *don't let him go.*
Do you understand?'

'No,' said Tom. 'Why—'

'Never mind why. Please, for once, just do it.' She
headed for the telephone.

Tom shrugged. He never would understand his wife.

The Maritime Museum was a rectangular red-brick building with a balcony running round the outside. The window
frames were painted dingy blue. Inside, Dylan glimpsed
machines, a lifeboat.

Admission free. In the entrance hall was an aquarium,
with fish and crabs. Lucky poked his head out of Dylan's
jacket and stared, entranced. Spotting an attendant, Dylan
pushed the kitten back down, and went upstairs.

No sign of her yet. Kate. Groups of visitors moved
around the exhibits. Families, mostly.

There were full-size boats, and models in cases. The
doors and cases, even some of the boats, were painted the
same shade of dingy blue; there were rows of chairs the
same colour.

Dylan sat down in a corner facing an old farm cart. He
looked at his watch: 11.04. She was late.

He waited. Several times he thought he saw her. All these
people passing and none of them the right one.

11.09. Perhaps she wasn't coming. Perhaps she'd decided
she didn't want anything to do with him.

Then, suddenly, she was there. She was wearing jeans
and a brightly patterned shirt. Dylan gazed at her,
thinking, she's my mother, she gave me away, she's a cow,
she looks like me, if only I could make her like me.

All he could find to say was, 'I like your shirt.'

'Thanks.' She sat down beside him, clutching her bag on
her lap, fiddling with the strap. 'Sorry I'm late. I couldn't
get away. And I'm sorry we have to meet here. Only my
children—my other children—don't know about you.'

'What are they called?' asked Dylan.

'Polly, she's fifteen, and Gareth. He's sixteen.'

My brother and sister, thought Dylan. They don't know I exist.

They waited as a family moved slowly past, the man explaining points of interest to the children, who looked bored. 'I want an ice cream,' announced the littlest.

'Come on,' said Kate. 'Let's walk.'

Outside it was warm in the noontime sun. They turned left, towards the docks, their feet keeping in step; but silent.

They passed the statue of Dylan Thomas in the square. A small boy was sitting on the poet's lap to be photographed. 'Was it after him you called me Dylan?'

Kate laughed. 'Bless you, no. *Bob* Dylan. Your—father— had all his records, he used to play them to me.'

There was a strong smell of frying onions coming from the steak house.

'Who was my father?' asked Dylan.

Kate started to say something, hesitated, sighed. At last she said, 'His name was John. I never told him about you. He was leaving, going to England.'

'Why didn't you go with him?'

'Oh, Dylan, I'm sorry, it wasn't like that. There were the children, and there was Colin—my husband, and I couldn't have left Swansea. This is my home.'

They walked over the footbridge, the heavy metal gate banging to behind them. The boats sat still in their reflections.

'It was—one of those things,' said Kate.

Dylan swallowed, staring hard at the water. One of those things. An accident.

Suddenly Kate cried out. Dylan turned. She was staring at his chest. Looking down he saw the kitten pushing his head out, blinking the sleep from his eyes.

'This is Lucky,' said Dylan.

She was still staring, mouth open.

'Don't you like him?' asked Dylan.

'Oh—yes—of course—it was just seeing it so suddenly.'

Lucky climbed upwards and perched on Dylan's

100

shoulder. I'm not sure I like her, thought Dylan. I don't have to like her.

They walked on round the harbour basin. To the right, behind blocks of flats, rose the hills; to the left the sky was light from the sea. A big cruiser creamed by, and one by one set the other boats dancing at their moorings.

People looked at them as they passed, pointing at the kitten. Kate was agitated, continually looking round. 'I keep thinking I see someone I know,' she said. 'It's not for myself, you understand. And you look so much like me.'

She glanced round at him, smiling nervously. 'I've wondered so often what you were like.'

They were almost the same height.

'Was my father tall?' asked Dylan.

'Not very. About five eight.'

'My dad's six foot. I always thought I'd be as big as him.'

Kate looked puzzled. 'Didn't they—your parents—didn't they tell you that you were adopted?'

Dylan shook his head. 'I found a letter. From a social worker.'

Lucky changed shoulders.

'*Found* a letter?' She was looking at him hard. Dylan was conscious of his unwashed face, the dirt under his fingernails, the clothes he'd slept in.

She stopped. 'Dylan—where are your parents?'

He was silent.

'Are they in Swansea?' she persisted.

He hesitated, thought of inventing some story, then made up his mind. 'I ran away.'

'Oh God.' She closed her eyes a moment. 'Where are you staying?'

'I'm sleeping in a cowshed.'

'Oh God,' she said again. '*You're sleeping rough?* Dylan, why? Aren't they good to you?'

He shrugged.

'I thought—' She stopped. 'I always thought it would be the best for you; the agency said they'd found a really nice family . . .'

101

'And best for you?' said Dylan.

She winced. 'If it had been up to me—but Colin wouldn't let me keep you . . . '

Dylan watched two seagulls squabbling over some food.

'You must let me help you,' she said. 'I can't ask you to come and stay with us, you understand that, don't you? Colin wouldn't hear of it, and I don't know what I'd say to Polly and Gareth. If only I could think of someone you could stay with . . . But let me give you some money . . . '

She started fumbling for her purse.

'No, thank you,' said Dylan. 'I don't need any money. I don't need anything.'

She stood there, the open purse in her hands.

'I think I'd better be going,' he said.

'No, don't go—Dylan—at least let me buy you some lunch.'

'No, thank you,' he said. 'I'm not hungry.'

'Don't go. I can't let you go.'

'You can't stop me.' He put one hand up to steady the kitten on his shoulder, turned on his heel and walked away.

Without any conscious decision, he headed back to the farmhouse. It was where he needed to be.

The derelict buildings, huddled in the bottom of the valley, were bathed in light. They looked sharp-edged, almost as if they were pulsing.

Dylan pushed through the brambles and stood in the doorway. The rubble lay ankle-deep in the decay of old fire and long time. Tendrils of ivy reached from the ruined chimney-stack to brush his face. Above, where upstairs used to be, the door to nothing swung on rusty hinges.

There was a sound of someone crying from above. Slowly, drawn despite himself, Dylan moved forward. To the foot of the stairs. Where no staircase was. And though he could see nothing but empty air where he trod, he was moving upwards. Slowly, from step to step, till he went through the door and stood in a bedroom.

There was Geraint, by the window, grim-faced; Beth lying in bed, staring at the ceiling; the little boy in the corner, endlessly piling three bricks on top of each other and knocking them down again; a tiny baby, red-faced and crumpled, noisily asleep in a crib.

A woman entered, walked over to the crib. She stooped down, wrapped the baby in a blanket, then picked it up. For a moment she stood, the baby in her arms; then she went out. In the corner, the child knocked the bricks down again.

Dylan was suddenly furiously angry. He raised his fist and crashed it against the door.

With a sudden crack the rusty hinges gave and the door toppled. All around planks and timbers were crashing downwards, and Dylan was falling with them. The house settled into its final decay; there was dust, and silence.

CHAPTER SIXTEEN
Wednesday 31 July: Afternoon

When Cerian got home Bea was waiting for her.

'Is Dylan with you?'

Cerian shook her head.

'Do you know where he is?'

Cerian, looking at her mother's face, again shook her head.

Bea sighed. 'Cerian, why didn't you tell me? Come on, you're not going to pretend you didn't know he'd run away.'

'I promised. It was a secret. I promised not to tell.'

'Tell me now.'

Cerian began the story with pride, but it shrivelled as she went. Somehow, with Bea's eyes fixed on her, the tale of her investigations seemed less impressive. She wasn't even sure that the meeting between Dylan and Catherine Elizabeth had been a total success.

'His poor parents,' said Bea. 'What they must have been going through.'

'But I promised not to tell,' said Cerian again. 'I couldn't betray a secret, could I?'

'Did you try to persuade him to tell me?'

' . . . No.' Cerian had to admit she had wanted to sort Dylan's problems out herself. It had all been so interesting, she hadn't wanted to think about what it meant, running away from home. She should have known, should have thought that Dylan was in danger and his parents would be terribly worried.

Then she heard footsteps in the hall, a heaven-sent opportunity to divert attention. 'I think Mamgu knew,' she said.

'Oh, did she?' said Bea grimly.

Mamgu came into the kitchen and met Bea's basilisk glare. 'Did she what?' she asked.

'Did you know Dylan is a runaway?'

'Yes, of course I knew. It was perfectly obvious if you only looked.'

Bea threw up a hand. 'Yes, I know, I didn't take enough notice. But why didn't you tell me?'

'Because I thought Dylan should have time and space to work things out for himself.'

'But what about his parents? They must have been worried sick.'

'Do them good,' said Mamgu unsympathetically. 'They shouldn't have made him want to leave home in the first place.'

Bea ground her teeth.

'What's all the fuss about?' asked Tom, drawn from the pottery by the sound of raised voices.

They ignored him. 'Where's Dylan sleeping?' Bea asked.

'Cwm Rhithiol,' said Cerian.

'The old farm?'

Cerian nodded.

'Dear God.'

Barkis, woken by the noise, hauled himself out from under the table and tried to climb on to Tom's lap.

'What *is* all this?' asked Tom.

'Do you think he might be there now?' asked Bea.

'Might be,' said Cerian.

'Right. Come with me.' Bea dragged Cerian out.

'Nobody ever tells me anything,' said Tom plaintively.

'Dear God,' said Bea again, contemplating the remains of the farmhouse.

'I think a bit more has fallen down,' said Cerian uncertainly.

'And Dylan's been sleeping *here*?'

Cerian nodded towards the sleeping-bag lying in a twisted heap by the doorpost.

'Don't go any further,' said Bea. 'It looks as if the whole

105

lot could fall down any moment. Well, he's not here now and, Heaven help me, his parents are on their way and he's been running tame in my house for a fortnight and I don't have any notion where he is.'

'I'll leave a note,' said Cerian. 'In case he comes back.'

'Just put that you want him to come round,' said Bea. 'I don't want him scared off.'

Cerian wrote the note and left it on the sleeping-bag. She looked a last time round the farmhouse. Something had changed. She was sure there was more rubble in the far corner. She shivered, then went out, glad to escape into the summer afternoon.

When they got back there were two strangers in the kitchen, looking up with strained faces of mingled hope and pain. The hope died when they saw only Bea and Cerian.

'These are Dylan's parents,' said Mamgu.

'Michael Wells,' said the man, getting up to shake hands. 'This is my wife, Linda.'

'I don't know how I can ever apologize—' began Bea.

'Please don't,' said Linda. 'At least now we know he's safe.'

'You got here very quickly,' said Bea.

'We were already getting ready to come when you phoned. Simon's—mother—rang the police, though she only knew he was somewhere in Swansea. Where is he?'

'He is all right, isn't he?' said Linda.

'Fine,' said Cerian. 'At least, he was yesterday. But I'm afraid I don't know where he is now. Shall I go and look for him? I can take my bike.'

'We'll all go,' said Bea. 'The more eyes, the better. We'll split up, take the car and the van—and your car, Michael?'

'Okay,' said Michael. 'Shall we arrange to meet somewhere?'

'By St Mary's,' said Tom. 'We should be able to stop there a few minutes. It's—ten past three now, shall we meet at five?'

'I'll come with you,' said Mamgu to Linda, 'so you don't get lost.'

The two cars and the van moved away in different directions. Cerian thought a moment, then swung her leg over her bike and set off downhill. If she was in Dylan's shoes she'd be down by the sea.

For a while she rode up and down the sea front. From the cycle path she had a good view of the beach: but she didn't see Dylan.

Dylan was saved by the kitten. He lay stunned under the heap of rafters and floorboards that had fallen with him. The kitten roused him, struggling out of the neck of his shirt, needle claws piercing his skin.

Alternately squeaking and sneezing, Lucky wriggled upwards, hauling himself out to the open air. Dylan, his eyes and nose and mouth clogged with dust, pushed blindly behind, squeezing through gaps, or where there were none, battering at the debris with head, shoulders, arms, feet.

At last, coughing and spluttering, he was free. He rubbed his sleeve over his face, trying to wipe away the grime, but only made things worse. His eyes watering, he peered round to find Lucky.

The kitten was in the doorway. Fur all over the place, he had changed from black and white to grey. His pink tongue showed as he licked a paw and wiped at his face, then sneezed.

Dylan clambered over the debris, picked up the kitten and carried him out. Behind him there was a sickening thud as a great rafter arrowed downwards and slammed into the dust. And with a sullen roar the rest of the roof fell in.

Lucky seemed unhurt. Dylan was too dirty to find out how much he himself was hurt. Shuddering with shock, his one idea was to get away.

He went downhill, towards the beach. On the way, he passed the prison, which is where he supposed he'd end up, once the police caught him.

If he hadn't stolen that money . . . But he had, and now most of it was spent and he couldn't give it back.

He cuddled Lucky in his arms and went on towards the sea, thinking he could wash all the dirt off with a swim. But the tide was out, and the sea an infinite distance away across shoals of glistening mud.

Standing hesitating, he became aware of the stares of passers-by. He must move: he turned left, towards the marina.

The grey bulk of the Leisure Centre gave him an idea. If he could get into a changing-room without anyone noticing him there would be showers . . .

He slipped in while the attendant was diverted trying to count a jostling crowd of Brownies.

Opposite the badminton court was a changing-room, mercifully empty. He put the kitten down, then walked under the shower without undressing, sighing with relief as the hot water flooded down through his hair, over his face. Then he took his clothes off and showered again.

The kitten needed a wash too. He could never lick all that dust off. Dylan picked Lucky up and held him firmly under the shower, despite loud squeaks of protest. So that, thought Dylan, is what a drowned rat looks like. The kitten seemed minute with his fur in flat streaks.

There were no towels, but there was an electric hand dryer. Dylan gave the kitten a blow dry, then put his wet clothes on and went out into the sunshine.

Cerian decided to check out the pedestrian precinct where the others, in cars, wouldn't be able to go. She parked her bike and went into the Quadrant Centre. It was stiff with people and she had to push her way through. Even if Dylan were there she'd be unlikely to see him.

She stopped for a breather by a boutique which had a sale on. There were some T-shirts she liked, half-price, a black one with green parrots . . . Pulling herself together, she turned into the market. It was a few minutes after four and the stalls were starting to pack up. Then she thought she saw Dylan in the distance, ran down the aisles, bumping into people; but it wasn't him.

She was haunted by the feeling that she kept missing him, that each time she went away from somewhere he would appear behind her. She stopped by a flower stall, trying to look in all directions at once.

'Can I help you?' An old lady sat behind the stall almost hidden in flowers; in front of them shiny black packs of laverbread and apricot heaps of cockles.

'Sorry,' said Cerian. 'I didn't see you there. I'm looking for someone—a boy, fair-haired, wearing jeans.'

The old lady shrugged. 'They all look the same to me. Here, have some cockles, fresh Penclawdd cockles.'

'No thanks,' said Cerian. She decided to go back to the beach and ask there.

But the first people she asked shook their heads. Come on, she muttered, call yourself an investigator? You'll have to manage a better description than that. Then she had an idea, and the next people she asked, 'Have you seen a boy with a kitten?'

And after a few attempts a girl said, 'Yes.'

'Where?'

The girl thought for a moment. 'I think he was going that way. Yes, towards the marina.'

'How long ago?'

She shrugged. 'A bit.'

Cerian looked at her watch. Ten to five. She could go after Dylan straight away, but then she might miss him, and anyway she wasn't sure what she would say. She hadn't meant to betray his secret.

Best if she went to fetch the others. She swung her leg over her bike.

Dylan was sitting on a bollard watching a big posh cruiser manoeuvring into the lock. The man at the wheel was wearing a yachting cap and a bristling moustache and kept yelling at the crew, who ran around with fenders and boathooks. Eventually they moored it in the right place and the lock gates closed.

Dylan was beginning to dry off, apart from his jeans, and the various cuts and grazes had stopped bleeding. Lucky was playing by his feet, disembowelling a sweetpaper. Suddenly his fur stood on end and he turned sideways, back arched. Dylan looked round; saw Barkis, grunting, bearing down on him. Behind the dog were Cerian and Tom and Bea and Mamgu. And his parents.

He had finished with running away. He stood up and faced them.

CHAPTER SEVENTEEN

Thursday 1 August

That night Dylan slept in a bed. He wasn't sure he liked it; he missed the starlight.

It was Mamgu who insisted, looking at the dark smudges of exhaustion under Dylan's eyes, that they should all stay the night and 'talk about things in the morning'. Linda accepted gratefully and fussed round Dylan like a mother hen, saying, 'So long as I've got you back', and 'Tomorrow, we'll talk about it tomorrow'. Michael said hardly a word.

Bea, declaring it was her turn to get dinner, produced an Indian takeaway. Dylan could barely swallow, just pulled at lumps of naan bread.

By half past eight he was in bed, tucked up on the sofa in Mamgu's sitting-room. Linda came to kiss him goodnight. Dylan was asleep before she was out of the room.

But it was not a restful sleep. Disturbed by the intermittently hushed voices of grown-ups going to bed, he drifted into dreams. Over and over again he dreamt that he climbed the staircase that wasn't there and pushed open the door from nowhere. On the other side he saw now Beth clutching a piglet, now Kate with her purse open in her hands, now Tom in tears as he slowly pulled the head off a gnome, now Michael, threatening, holding up the Swiss army knife.

At last he shook himself awake and looked at his watch. Ten past two. He tried his usual remedy, of making up fantasies, but none of them would work—not scoring for England in the World Cup (Was he English? Was he Welsh?); not the tough guy with the secret sorrow carrying his rucksack off into the sunset; not his real mother, happy at being reunited, taking him to live in a mansion by the sea.

He had run out of dreams.

At last he slid into sleep again, till roused by Barkis who shouldered open the door and tried to get as much of his bulk as possible on to the sofa. He was heavy and he slobbered, but he was something to hug.

And then Cerian peeked round the door and brought him a cup of tea.

Dylan sat in the front room of Cerian's house, the room that was kept for best, so was never used because there was never anything good enough. He was, despite himself, still conscious of the new clothes his parents had brought to fetch him home. New everything.

Opposite him, on the sofa, Michael sat in silence.

Lucky, curled up on Dylan's shoulder, purred.

Michael took out his pipe and a tobacco pouch. 'I thought you'd given up,' said Dylan.

'I have.' Michael filled the pipe, struck a match, held it over the bowl till it almost burnt his fingers, puffed out a cloud of smoke, lit another match as the pipe went out again.

The silence stretched.

Linda came in, shut the door, went to sit beside her husband. 'All packed,' she said brightly.

Michael scraped out his pipe, laid it in an ashtray.

Dylan fondled the kitten's ears.

Linda looked round at Michael, but he was staring at the floor.

'Simon—' she began.

'My name's not Simon. It's Dylan.'

Linda paused. When she began again, she didn't call him anything. It was all about how much they cared for him, how upset they'd been.

Dylan didn't want to listen. He pictured the fastest speedboat in the marina, imagined leaping on board, roaring off, first stop Spain, then on through clouds of blinding spray to a tropical island with coconuts and booby birds.

Rubbish, he thought, and sank the boat. He reached into his pocket, took out the knife and carefully, so as not to disturb Lucky, laid it on the coffee table.

He looked up at his parents. Michael was fiddling with his pipe again. Linda, though, looked at the knife. 'Where did you get that?' she asked.

'I stole some money,' said Dylan. 'I broke into a car.'

There was a long silence. Then: 'We can fix that, can't we?' said Linda, looking at her husband.

He pursed his lips, sucked at his pipe, made no reply.

'At least we've found you,' said Linda. 'So long as we've got you back we can sort everything out. You'll promise to be a good boy in future, won't you?'

'How *did* you find me?' asked Dylan.

'Bea phoned yesterday morning,' said Linda. 'She saw your picture in the paper.' She paused, bit her lip. 'But we already knew you were somewhere in Swansea. The police had just been. They'd had a call from . . . your mother.'

Your mother. It was out. The words seemed to fly around the room, flapping their wings and screeching.

'Why didn't you *tell* me?' asked Dylan, glaring at Linda accusingly. 'Why didn't you tell me I was adopted?' Lucky, disturbed, jumped down.

Linda hesitated, made as if to speak, closed her mouth again, looked round once more at her husband.

There was a clinking sound as Michael knocked his pipe out in the ashtray. He cleared his throat, clenched the empty pipe between his teeth. 'That was my decision,' he said.

Dylan looked at him, startled.

Michael sighed. 'It was for the best,' he said. 'As things have turned out, I suppose it was a mistake. But I meant it for the best.'

'But why?' asked Dylan again.

Michael was avoiding his eyes. 'I knew what it was like,' he said, 'knowing your parents have abandoned you.'

'But—' Dylan didn't understand.

'I spent the first four years of my life in a children's home,' said Michael. 'Then I was fostered, different families, for a while. I went to live with your Grandma and Grandad when I was six. Eventually they adopted me.'

He fell silent. Linda stared at her knees.

Dylan felt confused. 'But . . . Uncle Richard and Aunt Isobel . . .'

'Are not blood relations of either you or me. I grew up . . .' He paused. 'I hoped I'd never have to tell you this . . . I grew up always feeling second best. Thinking that Richard and Isobel were favourites . . . Every time there was a row or my parents told me off, I was sure it was because I wasn't their real son.' He almost smiled. 'And I did behave very badly.'

Lucky discovered a box of paper hankies and started to pull them out, creating a cloud of bits of tissue.

'I didn't want you to feel like I did,' said Michael. 'I thought, if we didn't tell you . . .'

'And you found out you'd been wrong, didn't you,' Linda broke in. 'About your parents . . .'

Michael glanced at her. 'Hmmm.' He took refuge once more in his pipe, picking the strands of tobacco up with care, tamping them down. He dropped a match, still lit, into the ashtray. Dylan watched it burn till there was nothing left but a twist of charcoal and a brief puff of smoke.

'You see, once we had you . . .' said Michael. 'Of course you were much younger, only six weeks old when we got you . . . anyway, then I realized it didn't make any difference so far as we were concerned, the fact that you were adopted. You were our son. In fact, perhaps even more our son because we had the chance to choose you.' He half smiled. 'I got on much better with my parents after that.'

'But I didn't choose you,' said Dylan, aware he sounded rude and hostile, though what he really felt was confused.

'No.' Michael sighed. 'No, you're right. And I was wrong . . . I've made a lot of mistakes, said things I didn't mean, got cross at you when I was really cross over something else. But . . . ' He was staring at his feet, his voice scarcely audible. 'But you do have two parents who love you and want you and want the best for you. So—so perhaps you *could* choose us?'

Dylan hesitated. It was all too much to take in. He didn't know what to say. The silence seemed to go on for ever and the longer it lasted, the less he could think what to say.

Lucky had abandoned the tissues and was climbing the curtains, swinging there like Tarzan.

'I'm not sure I can cope with that cat,' said Linda, suddenly breaking the silence, her voice high-pitched.

Dylan looked up, panicked. 'No—'

'We'll find it a good home,' said his mother.

'No!' screamed Dylan, scrambling to his feet, grabbing Lucky and holding him close. 'Lucky's mine. Mine. Can't you understand that? I look after him. I won't part with him. Never. Do you understand?'

Michael stared at his son, standing bright-eyed, defiant. The usual parental remarks ('That's no way to talk to your mother' or 'You'll do as you're told') shrivelled on his lips.

'But animals are so messy,' said Linda.

'Life's messy,' said Michael.

He finally met his son's eyes. They exchanged an uncertain smile.

Dylan, Cerian and Barkis walked, one last time, over the fields to Cwm Rhithiol.

At the crest of the hill they paused. Dylan looked down over the swell of the fields, tawny in the evening sun, to the wide sweep of Swansea Bay. The tide was in and the light sparkled about the small boats chugging out to sea.

I love this place, he thought. It felt warm, familiar, like home.

Though now he was leaving, for London, which really was home.

Cerian heaved Barkis to his feet again and they went on down the track.

Dylan's rucksack was still lying in the cowshed. He picked it up, then followed the path through the weeds to the farmhouse door.

All the roof had fallen in now. Open to the sky, the house seemed empty. No ghosts.

'Has more of it fallen down?' asked Cerian.

Dylan nodded. 'I think I made it fall. There were the ghosts, you see.' He hesitated, not knowing how to explain, not sure if he wanted to. 'I thought it was them at first that made the roof fall in. Now I think it was me. I got so angry . . . '

'You saw the ghosts again?'

'I saw them every night. Though I'm not sure if they were really there or if they were inside my head . . . '

Cerian stared at him. 'I'm confused,' she said.

'So am I,' said Dylan.

Suddenly he grinned.

'What's the joke?' asked Cerian.

'Nothing.' It was just that he didn't feel angry any more. He felt—okay. Before lunch he had helped his dad do some work on the car and they had talked about cars and he had told Michael about the mini-rugby match and they had laughed and his dad had promised to go with him to see Arsenal play. And Linda had said she liked Lucky really, if only he wouldn't chase the birds. And now he was going home, not because he had to, but because he wanted to. His choice.

Lucky squirmed out of Dylan's shirt and jumped down.

'You will come back?' asked Cerian. 'Mum says you can come and stay in the holidays. And Dad says he'll make the soup and teach you how to pot.'

'Sounds great,' said Dylan.

Lucky pounced. Barkis twisted round to see the small, determined kitten scrambling up on to his back.

The St Bernard gave a long-suffering sigh: but his eyes looked pleased. Slowly his tail began to wag.

WOLF
Gillian Cross

Cassy has never understood the connection between the secret midnight visitor to her nan's flat and her sudden trips to stay with her mother. But this time it seems different. She finds her mother living in a squat with her boyfriend Lyall and his son Robert. Lyall has devised a theatrical event for children on wolves, and Cassy is soon deeply involved in presenting it. Perhaps too involved – for she begins to sense a very real and terrifying wolf stalking her.

THE FOX OF SKELLAND
Rachel Dixon

Samantha's never liked the old custom of Foxing Day – the fox costume especially gives her the creeps. So when Jason and Rib, children of the new publicans at The Fox and Lady, find the costume and Jason wears it to the fancy-dress disco, she's sure something awful will happen.

Then Sam's old friend Joseph sees the ghost of the Lady and her fox. Has she really come back to exact vengeance on the village? Or has her appearance got something to do with the spate of burglaries in the area?

FLOWER OF JET
Bell Mooney

It's the time of the miners' strike. Tom Farrell's father is branded with the word Tom most dreads; Melanie Wall's father is the strike leader. How can Tom and Melanie's friendship survive the violence and bitterness of both sides? Things are to grow far worse than they ever imagined, for Melanie and Tom discover a treacherous plot that could destroy both their families. And they have to act fast if they're going to stop it.

MIGHTIER THAN THE SWORD
Clare Bevan

Adam had always felt he was somehow special, different from the rest of the family, but could he really be a modern-day King Arthur, the legendary figure they're learning about at school? Inspired by the stories they are hearing in class, Adam and his friends become absorbed in a complex game of knights and good deeds. All they need is a worthy cause for which to fight. So when they discover that the local pond is under threat, Adam's knights are ready to join battle with the developers.

Reality and legend begin to blur in this lively, original story about an imaginative boy who doesn't let a mere wheelchair get in his way of adventure.